FOR MANDY, IAN, ASTRID, AND THOR

ABOUT THIS BOOK

This book was edited by Andrea Spooner and art directed by Dave Caplan. The production was supervised by Bernadette Flinn, and the production editor was Lindsay Walter-Greaney. The text was hand-lettered by Greg Pizzoli.

 • Little, Brown and Company • Hachette Book Group • 1290 Avenue of the Americas, New York, NY 10104 • Visit us at LBYR.com • First Edition: May 2021 • Little, Brown and Company is a division of Hachette Book Group, Inc. • The Little, Brown name and logo are trademarks of Hachette Book Group, Inc. • The publisher is not responsible for websites (or their content) that are not owned by the publisher. • Library of Congress Cataloging-in-Publication Data • Names: Pizzoli, Greg, author, illustrator. • Title: Baloney and friends: going up! / Greg Pizzoli. • Description: First edition. • New York: Little, Brown and Company, 2021. • Series: Baloney and friends • Summary: "Baloney and friends continue their adventures that include creating a theme song, having a sleepover, using their imagination, and learning to appreciate the meaning of life"—Provided by publisher. • Identifiers: LCCN 2020022080 (print) • LCCN 2020022081 (ebook) • ISBN 9780759554801 (paper over board) • ISBN 9780759554818 (ebook) • Subjects: LCSH: Graphic novels. • CYAC: Graphic novels. • Friendship—Fiction. • Classification: LCC PZ7.7.P54 Bal 2021 (print) • LCC PZ7.7.P54 (ebook) • DDC 741.5/973—dc23 • LC record available at https://lccn.loc.gov/2020022080 • LC ebook record available at https://lccn.loc gov/2020022081 • ISBNs: 978-0-7595-5480-1 (paper over board), 978-0-7595-5481-8 (ebook), 978-0-316-59251-2 (ebook), 978-0-316-59253-6 (ebook) •
PRINTED IN CHINA • APS • 10 9 8 7 6 5 4 3 2 1

BALONEY

AND FRIENDS

GOING UP!

GREG PIZZOLI

LB

LITTLE, BROWN AND COMPANY

New York   Boston

TABLE OF CONTENTS

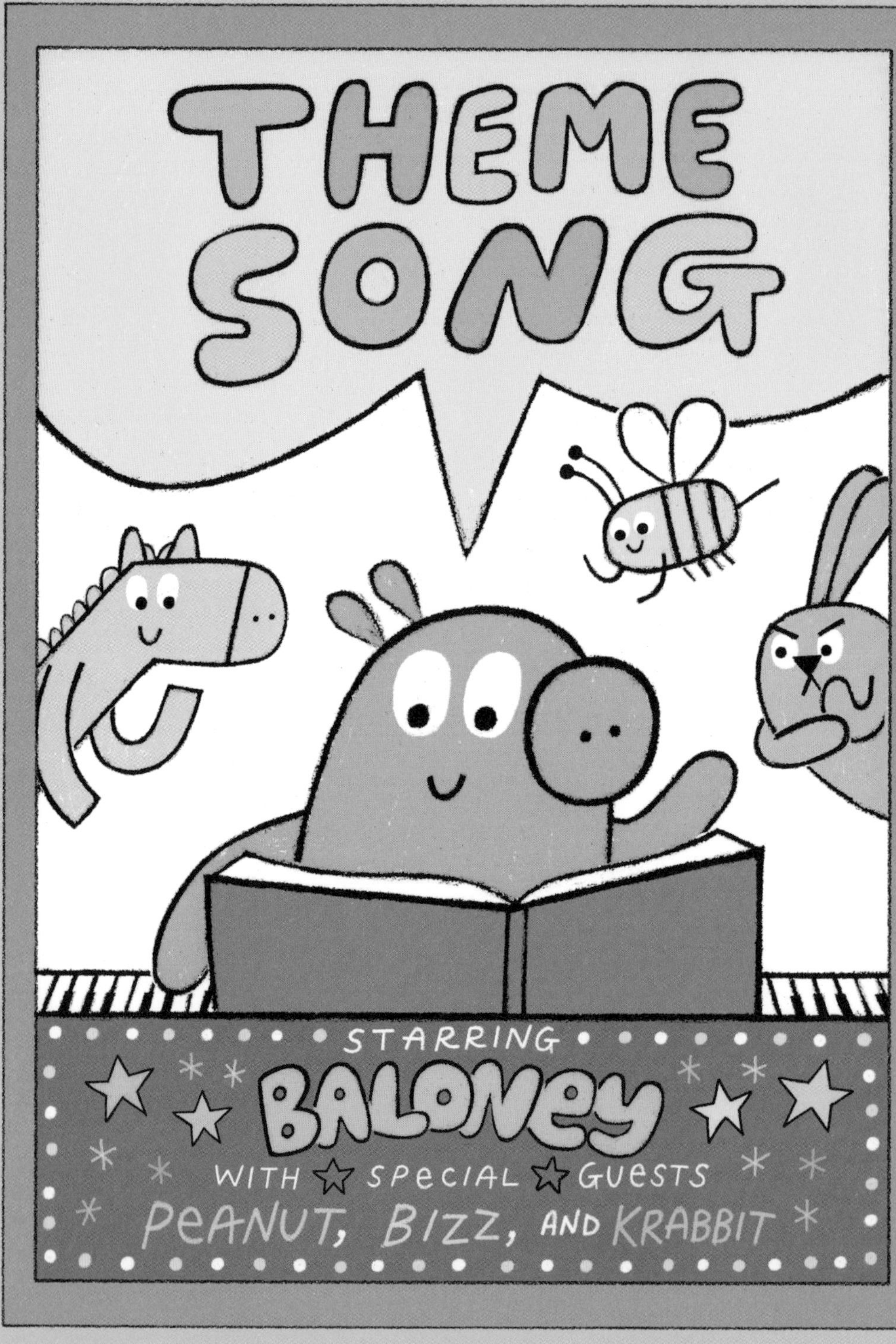
THEME SONG
STARRING
BALONEY
WITH SPECIAL GUESTS
PEANUT, BIZZ, AND KRABBIT

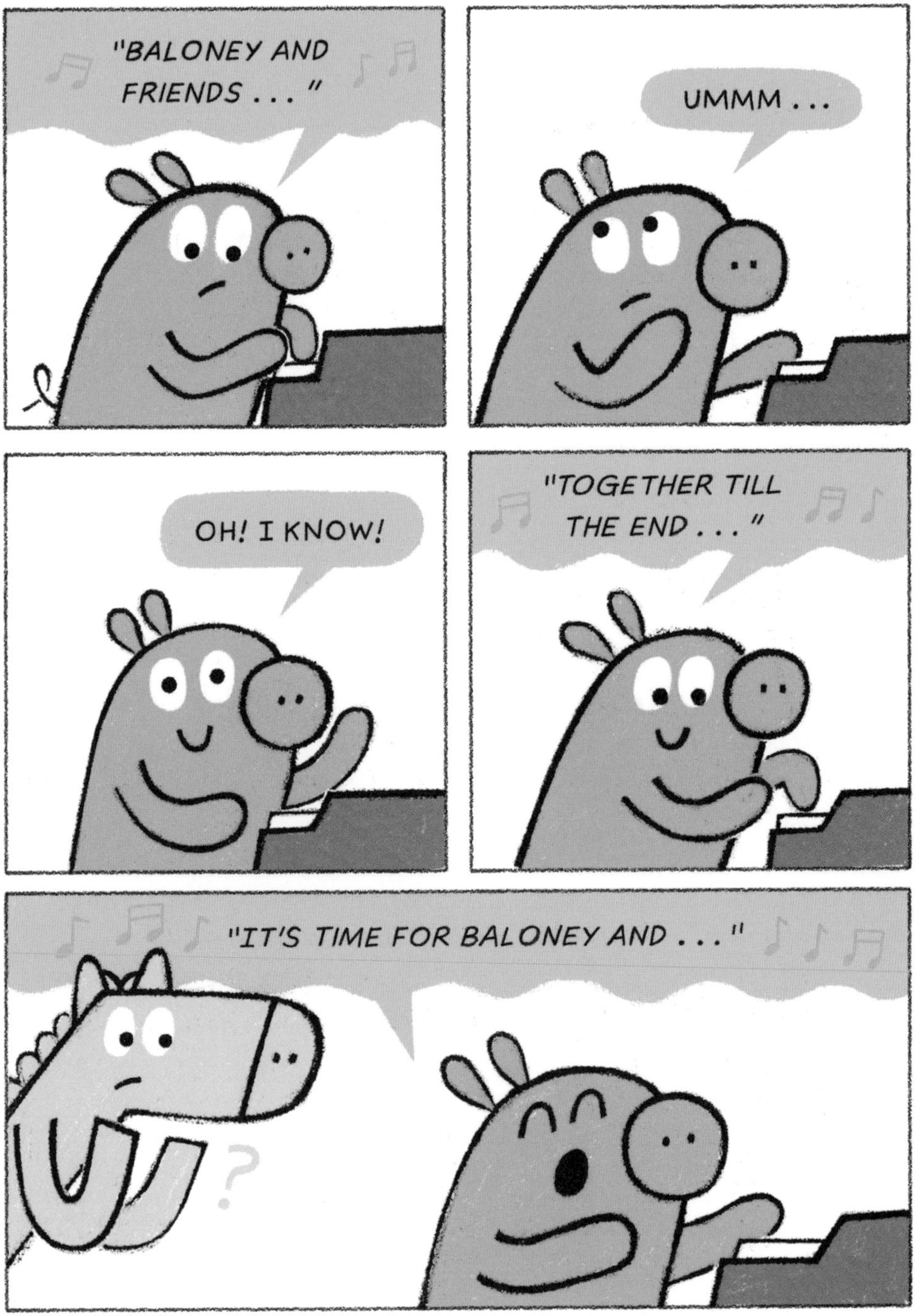
"BALONEY AND FRIENDS . . . "
UMMM . . .
OH! I KNOW!
"TOGETHER TILL THE END . . . "
"IT'S TIME FOR BALONEY AND . . . "
?

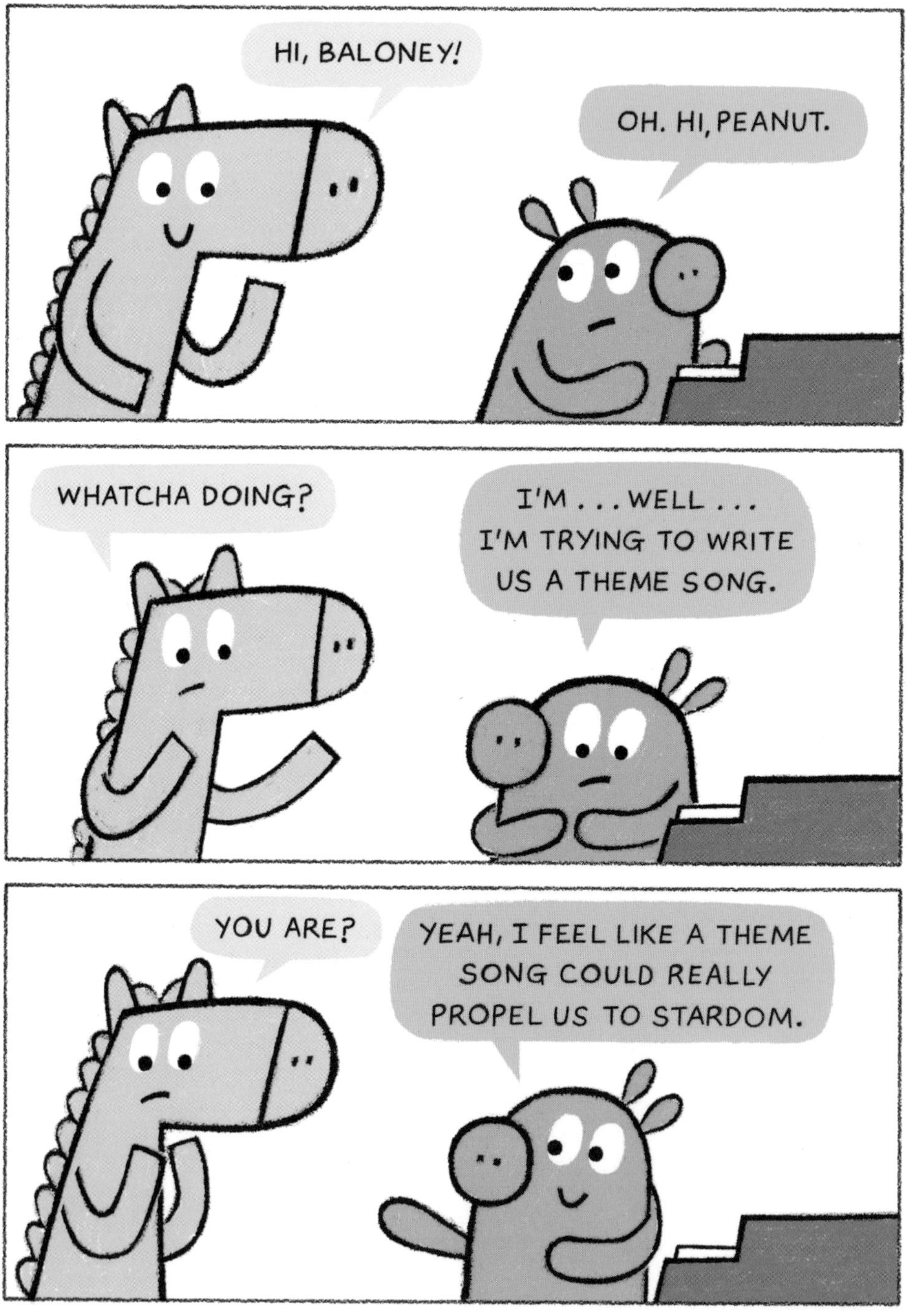
HI, BALONEY!
OH. HI, PEANUT.
WHATCHA DOING?
I'M . . . WELL . . . I'M TRYING TO WRITE US A THEME SONG.
YOU ARE?
YEAH, I FEEL LIKE A THEME SONG COULD REALLY PROPEL US TO STARDOM.

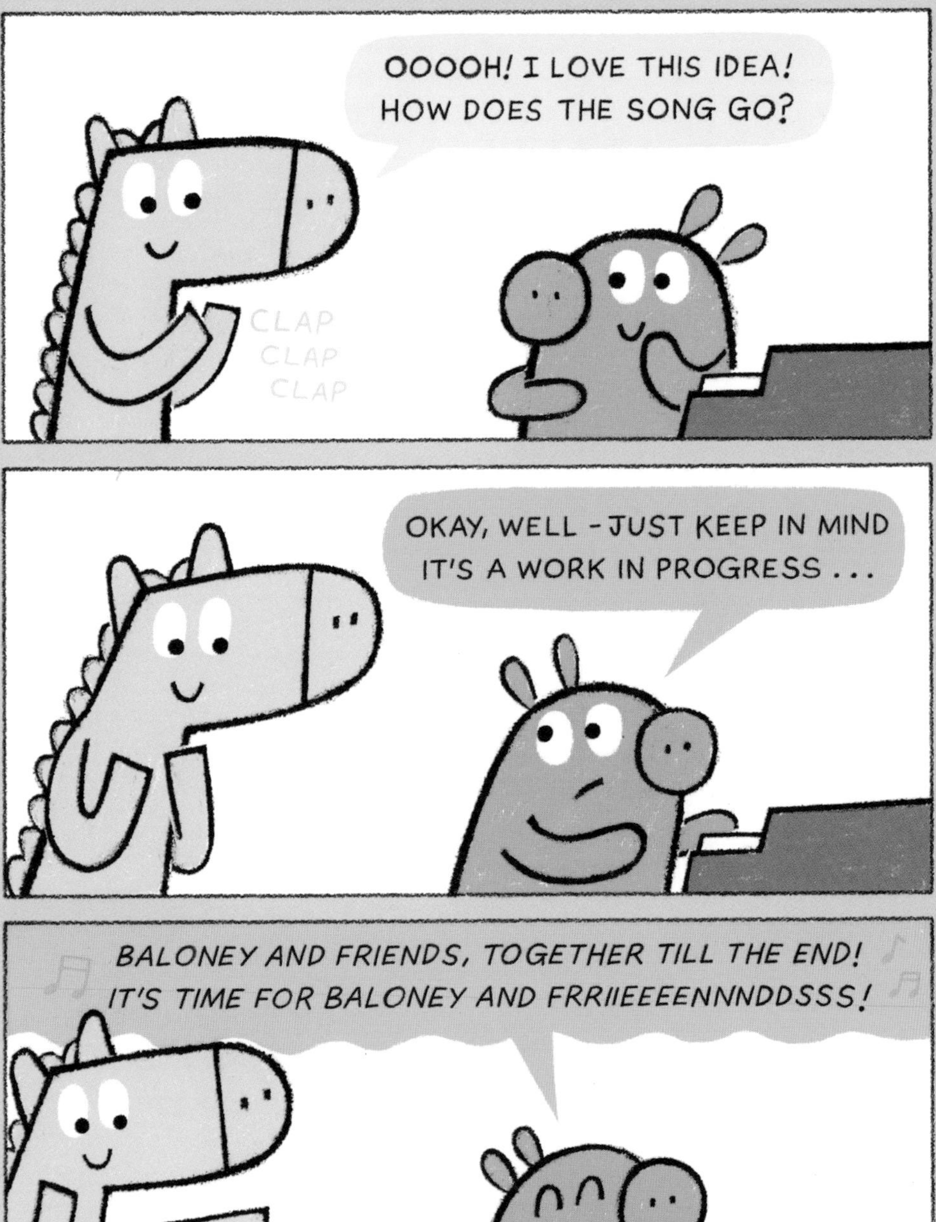
OOOOH! I LOVE THIS IDEA! HOW DOES THE SONG GO?
CLAP CLAP CLAP
OKAY, WELL - JUST KEEP IN MIND IT'S A WORK IN PROGRESS . . .
BALONEY AND FRIENDS, TOGETHER TILL THE END! IT'S TIME FOR BALONEY AND FRRIIEEEENNNDDSSS!

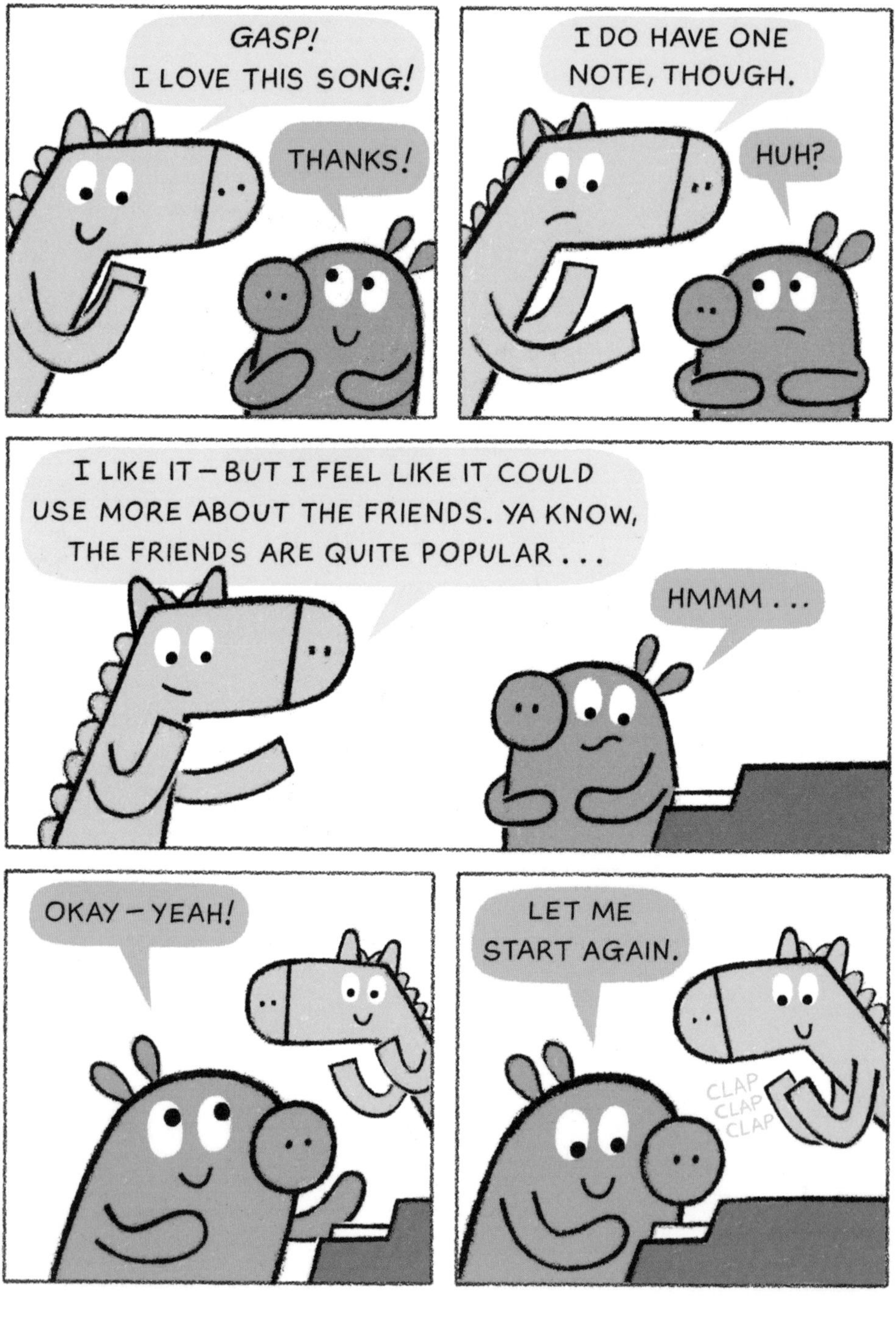
GASP!
I LOVE THIS SONG!
THANKS!
I DO HAVE ONE NOTE, THOUGH.
HUH?
I LIKE IT — BUT I FEEL LIKE IT COULD USE MORE ABOUT THE FRIENDS. YA KNOW, THE FRIENDS ARE QUITE POPULAR . . .
HMMM . . .
OKAY — YEAH!
LET ME START AGAIN.
CLAP
CLAP
CLAP

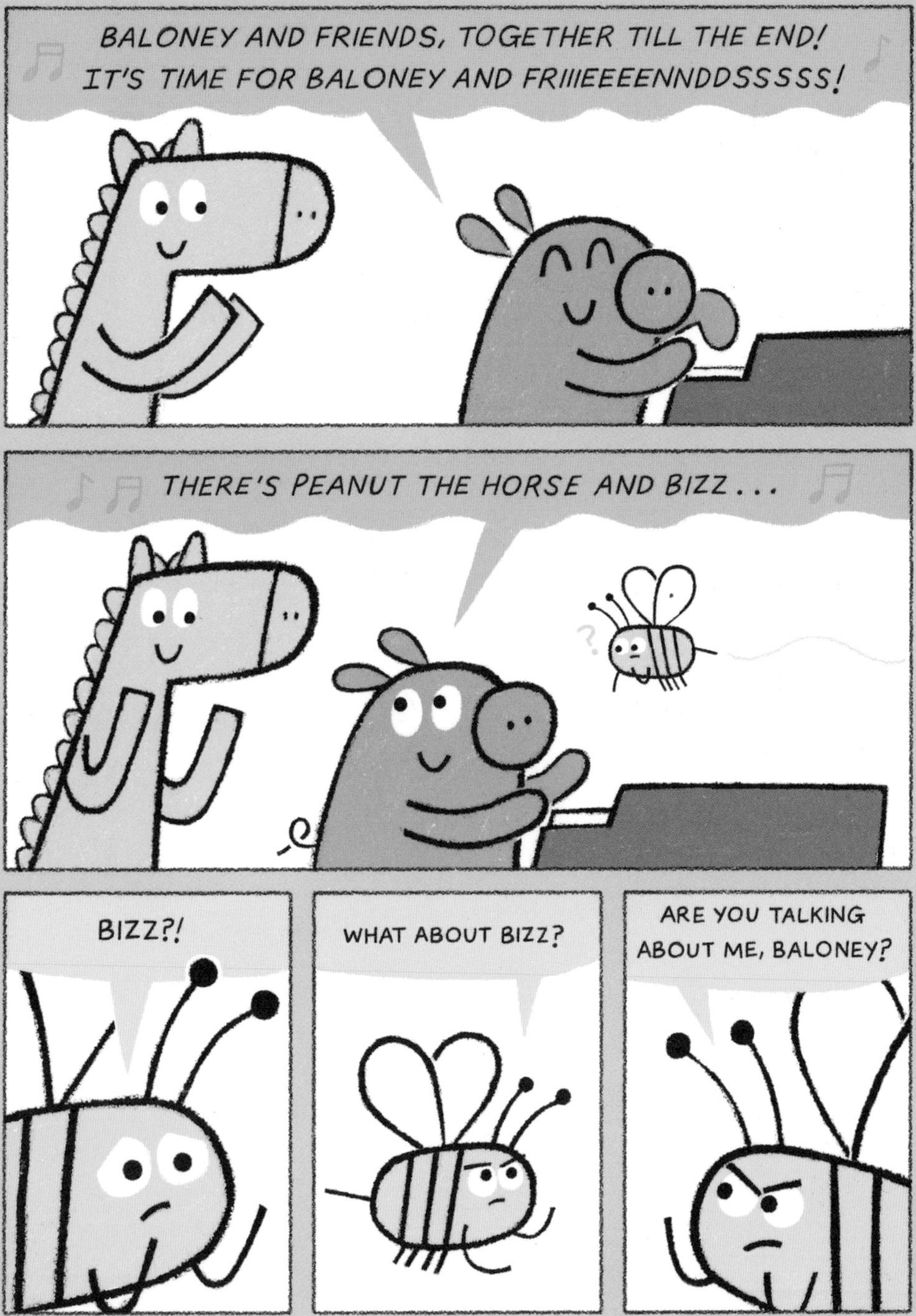
BALONEY AND FRIENDS, TOGETHER TILL THE END!
IT'S TIME FOR BALONEY AND FRIIIEEEENNDDSSSSS!
THERE'S PEANUT THE HORSE AND BIZZ . . .
BIZZ?!
WHAT ABOUT BIZZ?
ARE YOU TALKING ABOUT ME, BALONEY?

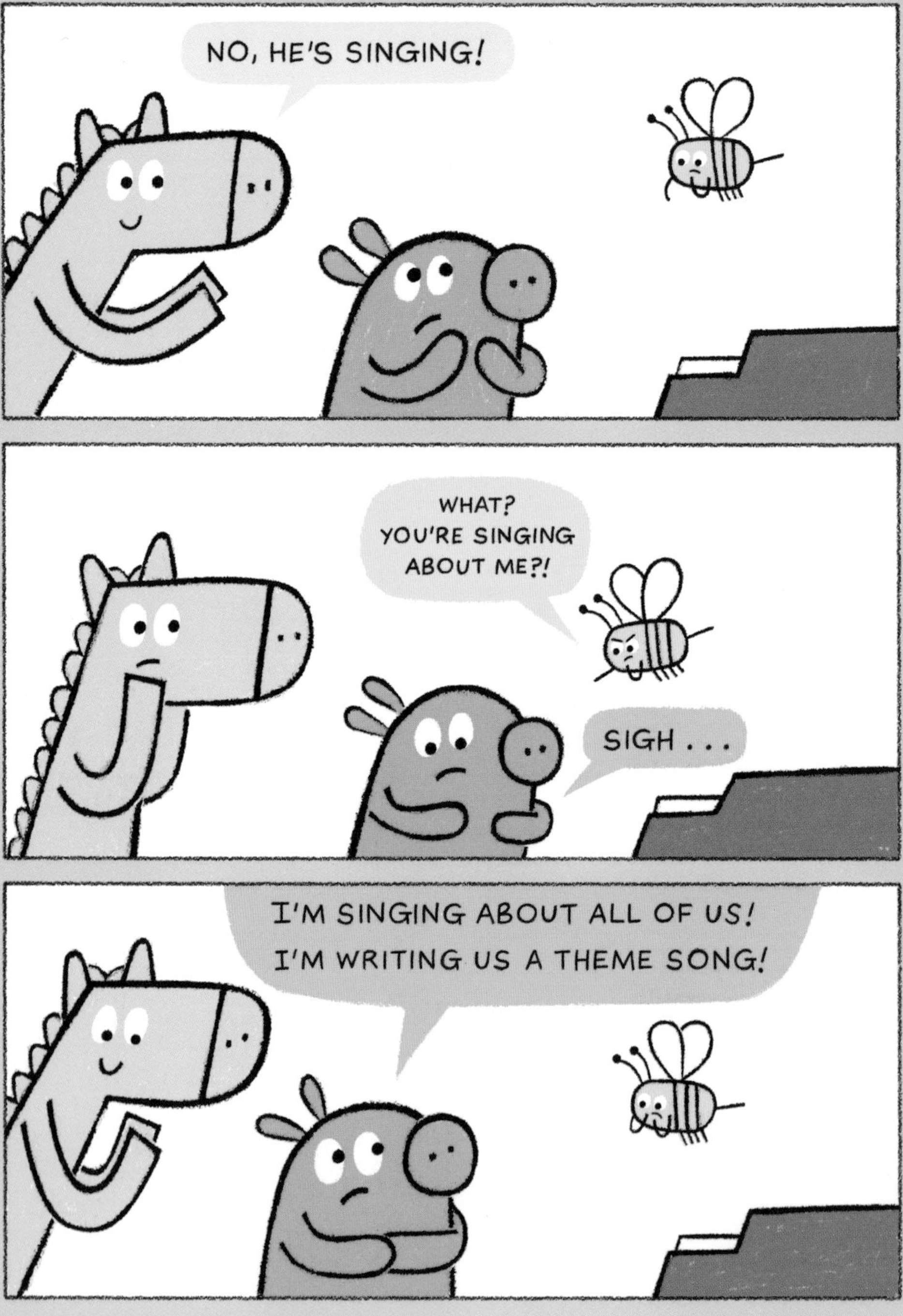
NO, HE'S SINGING!
WHAT? YOU'RE SINGING ABOUT ME?!
SIGH . . .
I'M SINGING ABOUT ALL OF US! I'M WRITING US A THEME SONG!

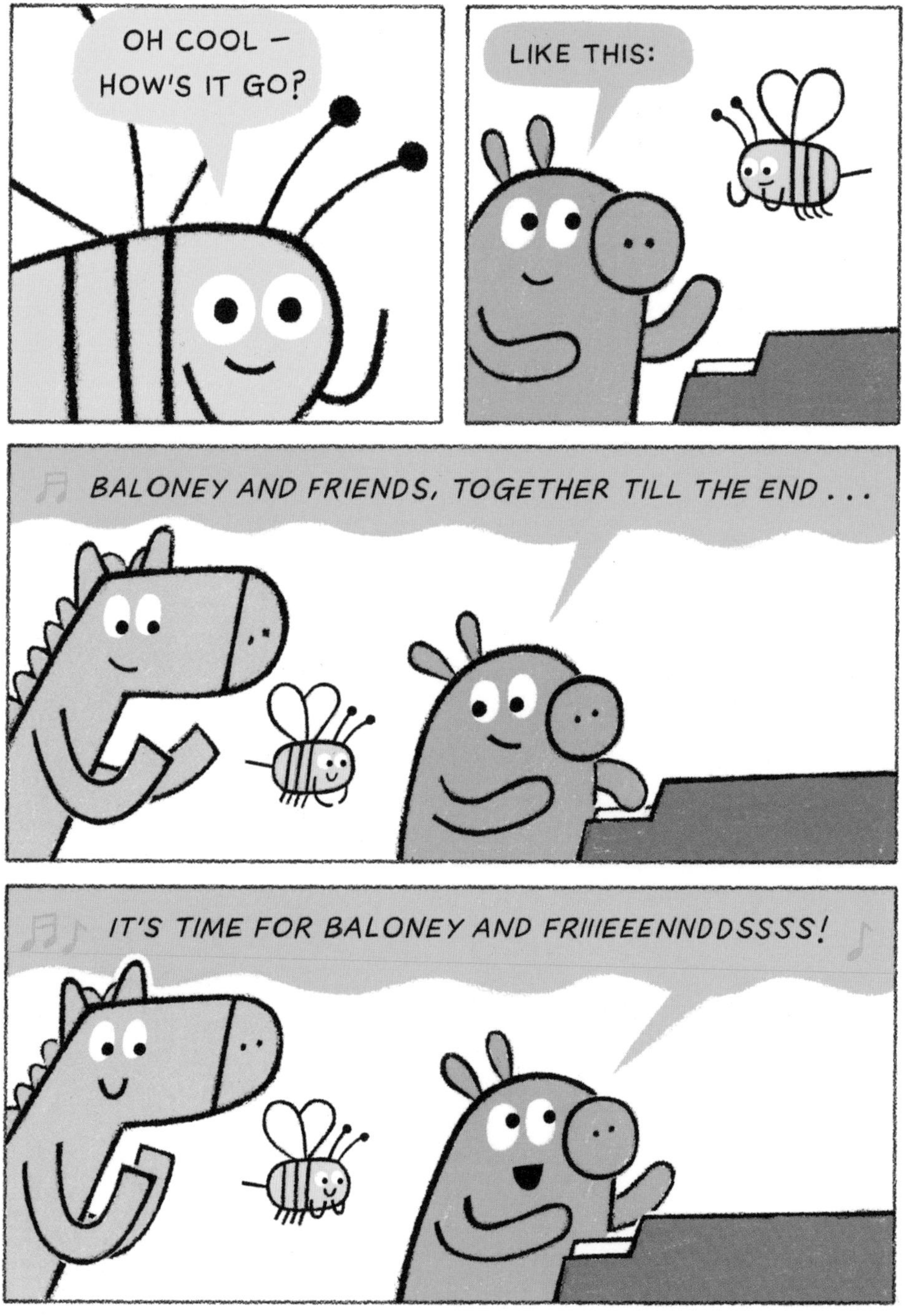
OH COOL — HOW'S IT GO?
LIKE THIS:
BALONEY AND FRIENDS, TOGETHER TILL THE END . . .
IT'S TIME FOR BALONEY AND FRIIIEEENNDDSSSS!

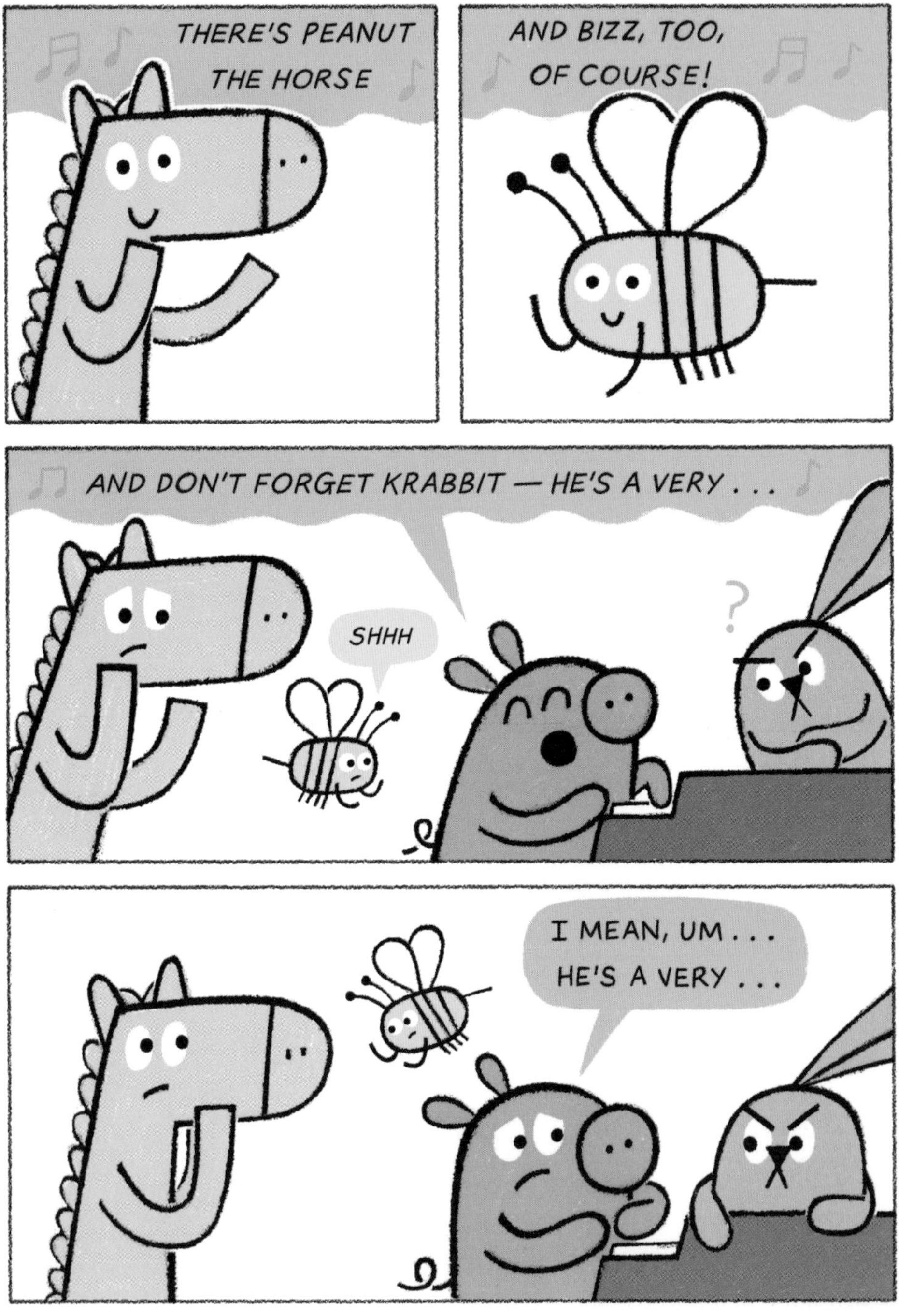
THERE'S PEANUT THE HORSE
AND BIZZ, TOO, OF COURSE!
AND DON'T FORGET KRABBIT — HE'S A VERY . . .
SHHH
?
I MEAN, UM . . . HE'S A VERY . . .

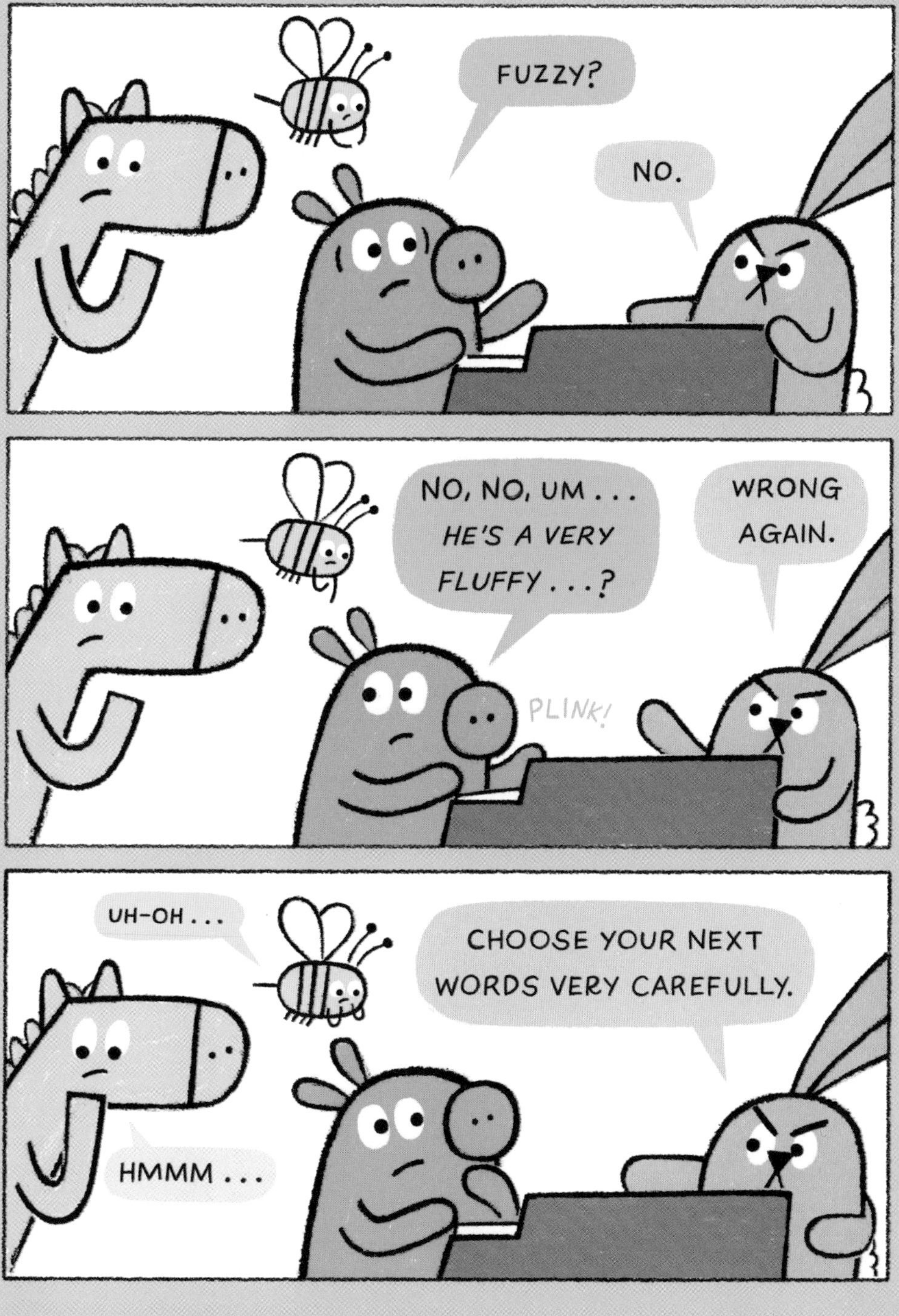
FUZZY?
NO.
NO, NO, UM . . . *HE'S A VERY FLUFFY . . . ?*
WRONG AGAIN.
PLINK!
UH-OH . . .
CHOOSE YOUR NEXT WORDS VERY CAREFULLY.
HMMM . . .

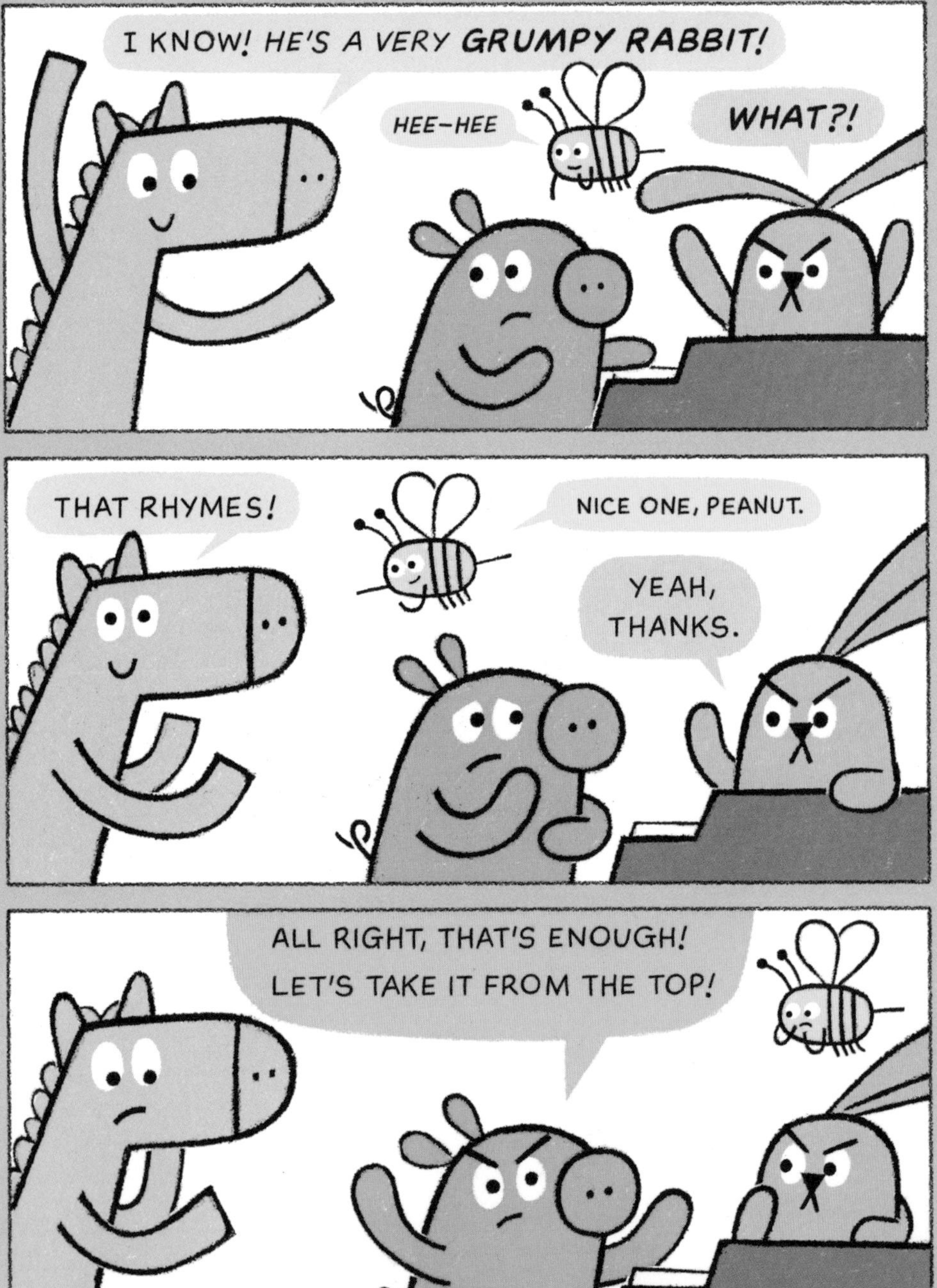
I KNOW! HE'S A VERY GRUMPY RABBIT!
HEE-HEE
WHAT?!
THAT RHYMES!
NICE ONE, PEANUT.
YEAH, THANKS.
ALL RIGHT, THAT'S ENOUGH! LET'S TAKE IT FROM THE TOP!

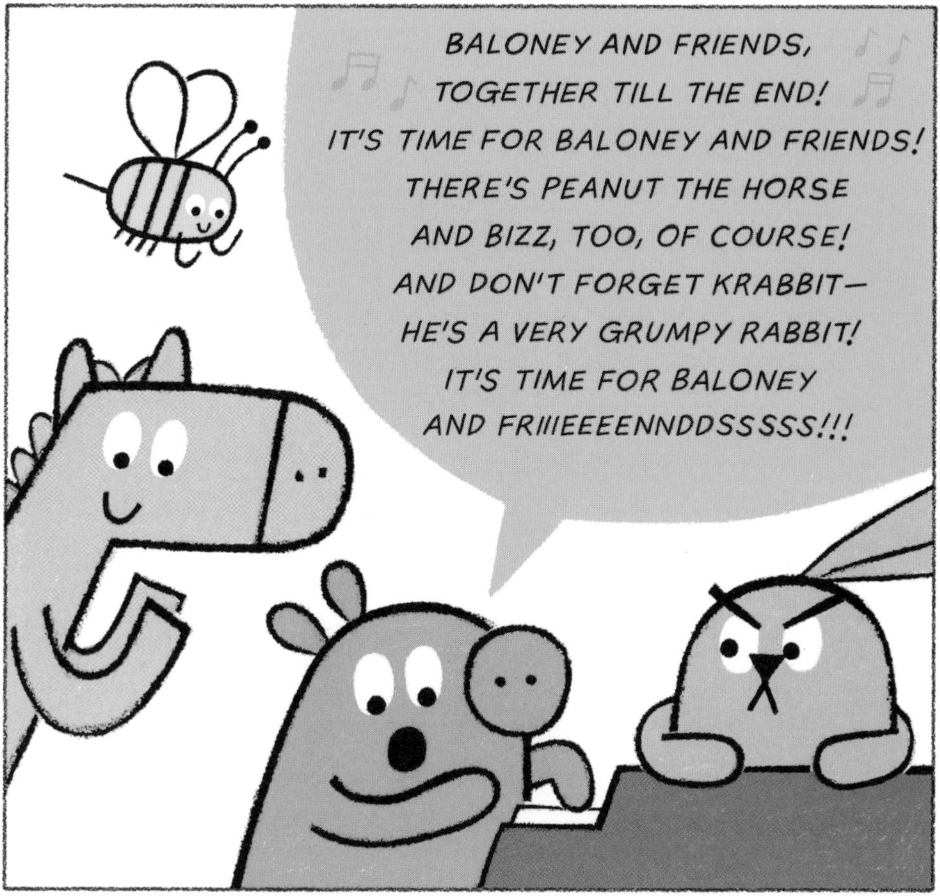
BALONEY AND FRIENDS,
TOGETHER TILL THE END!
IT'S TIME FOR BALONEY AND FRIENDS!
THERE'S PEANUT THE HORSE
AND BIZZ, TOO, OF COURSE!
AND DON'T FORGET KRABBIT—
HE'S A VERY GRUMPY RABBIT!
IT'S TIME FOR BALONEY
AND FRIIIEEEENNDDSSSSS!!!

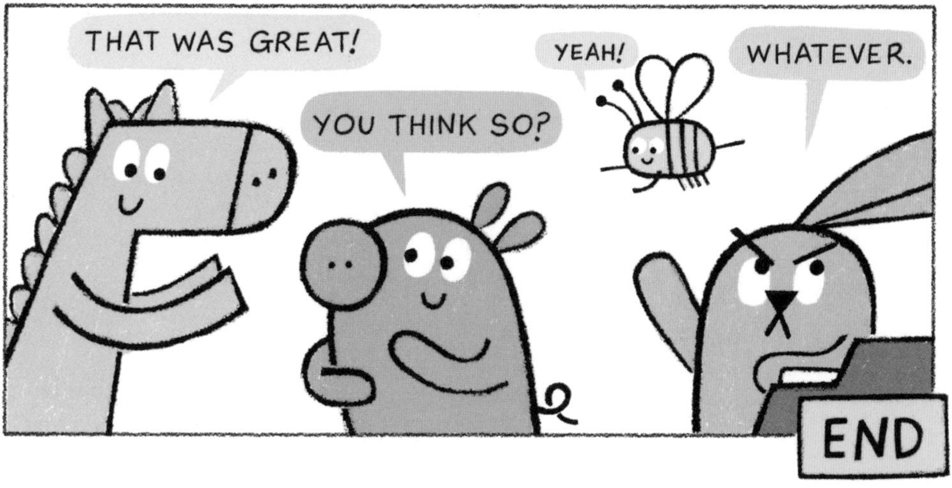
THAT WAS GREAT!
YOU THINK SO?
YEAH!
WHATEVER.
END

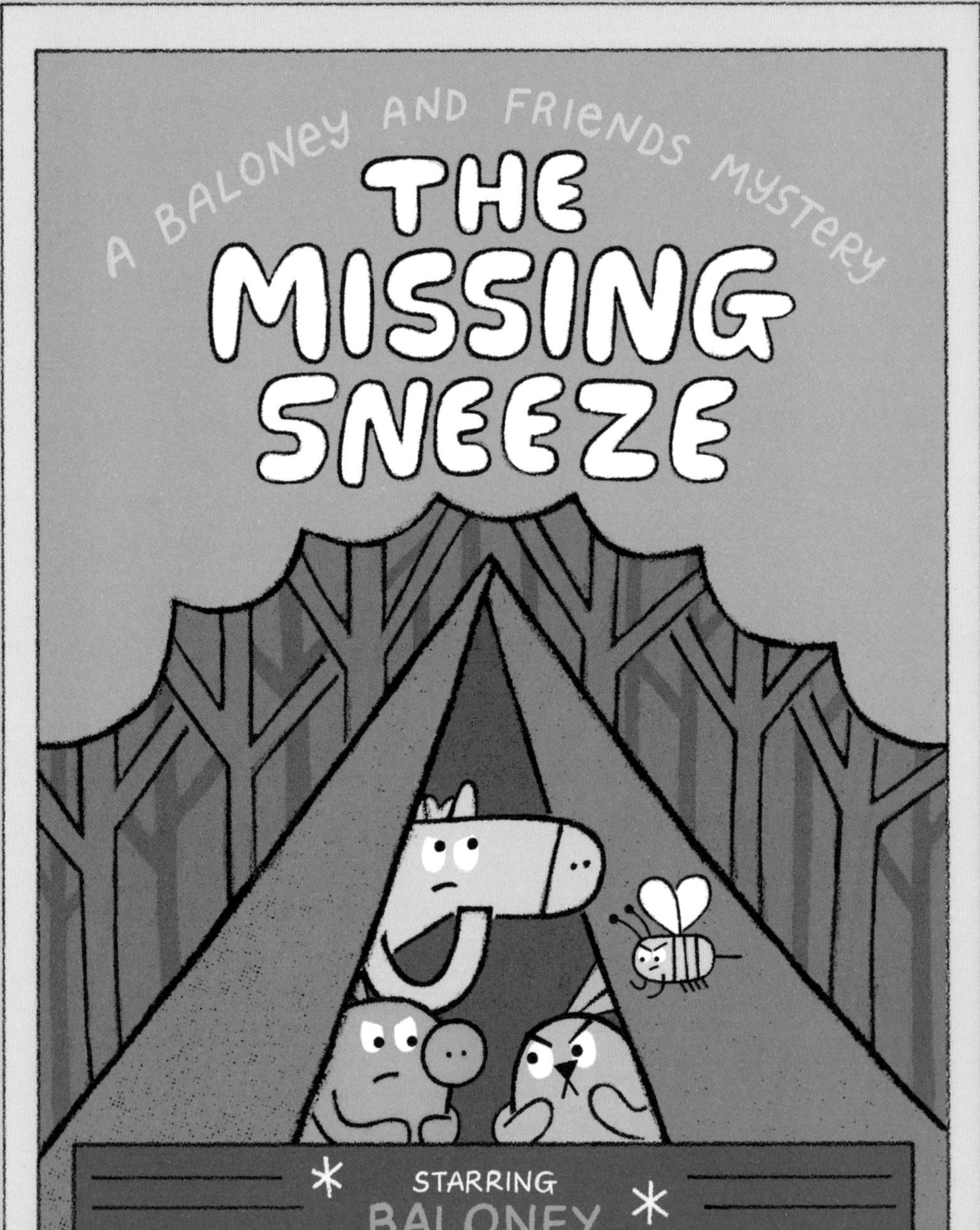
A BALONEY AND FRIENDS MYSTERY
THE MISSING SNEEZE
STARRING
BALONEY
WITH GUEST STARS
PEANUT, BIZZ, AND KRABBIT

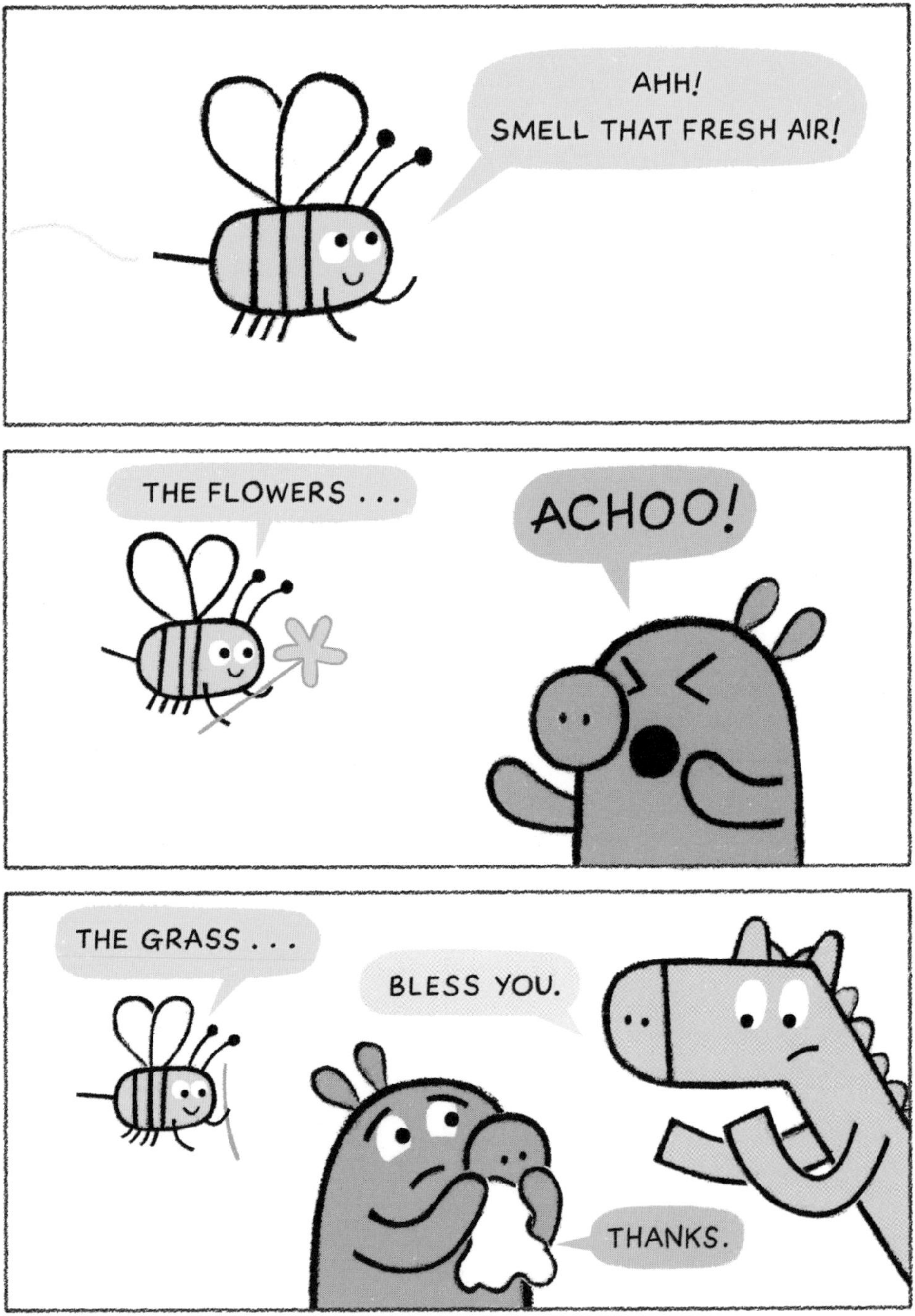
AHH!
SMELL THAT FRESH AIR!
THE FLOWERS . . .
ACHOO!
THE GRASS . . .
BLESS YOU.
THANKS.

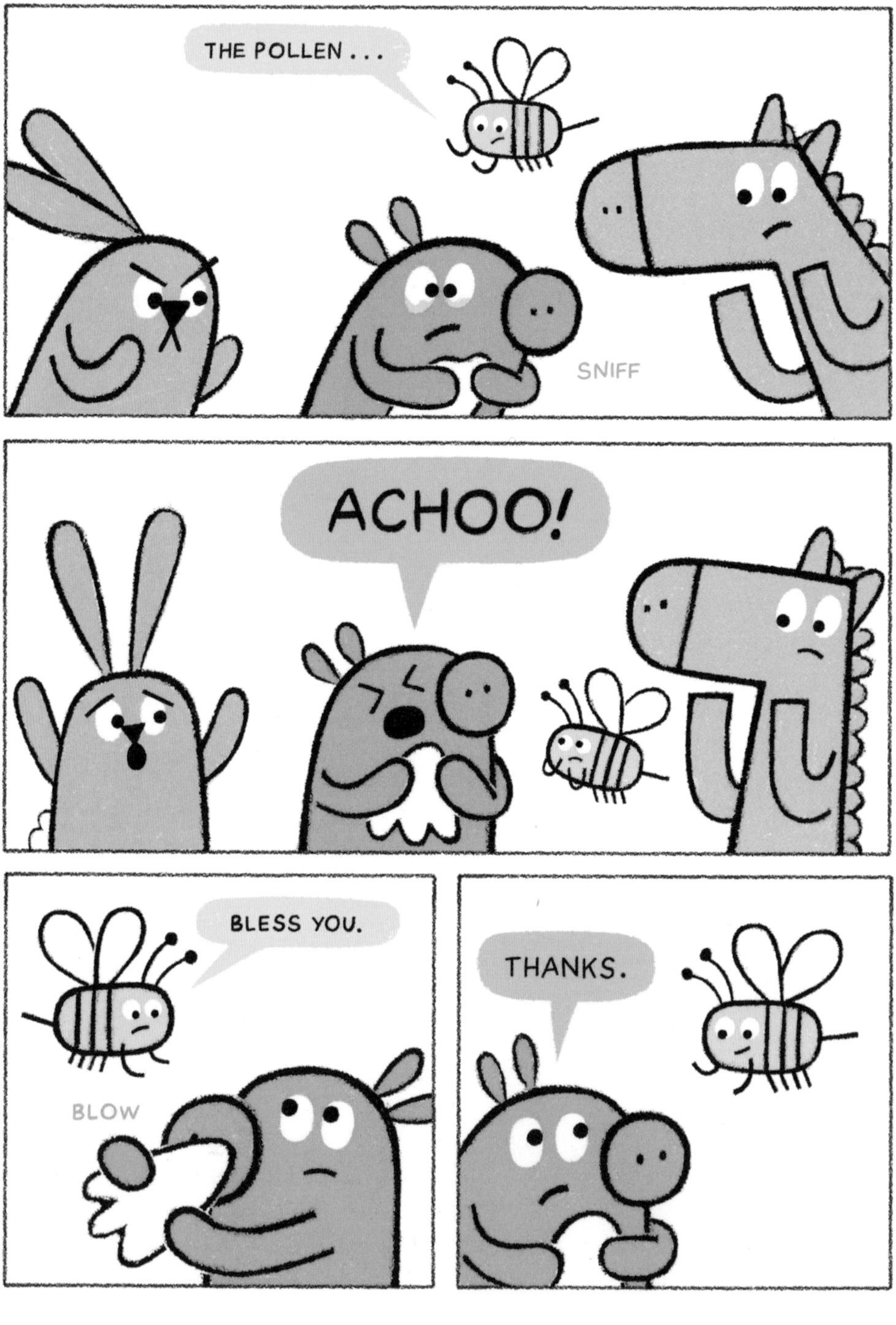
THE POLLEN . . .
SNIFF
ACHOO!
BLESS YOU.
BLOW
THANKS.

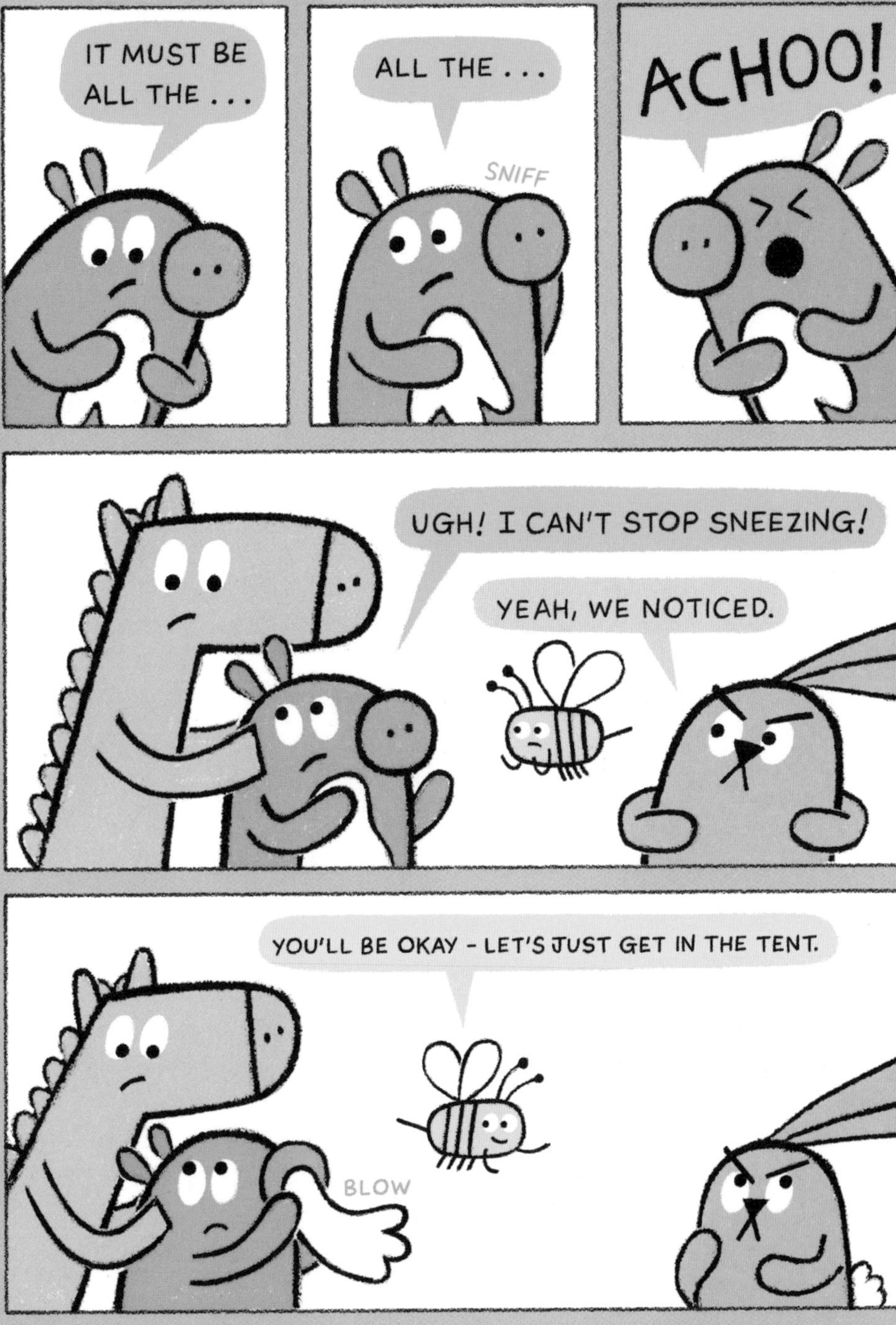
IT MUST BE ALL THE . . .
ALL THE . . .
SNIFF
ACHOO!
UGH! I CAN'T STOP SNEEZING!
YEAH, WE NOTICED.
YOU'LL BE OKAY - LET'S JUST GET IN THE TENT.
BLOW

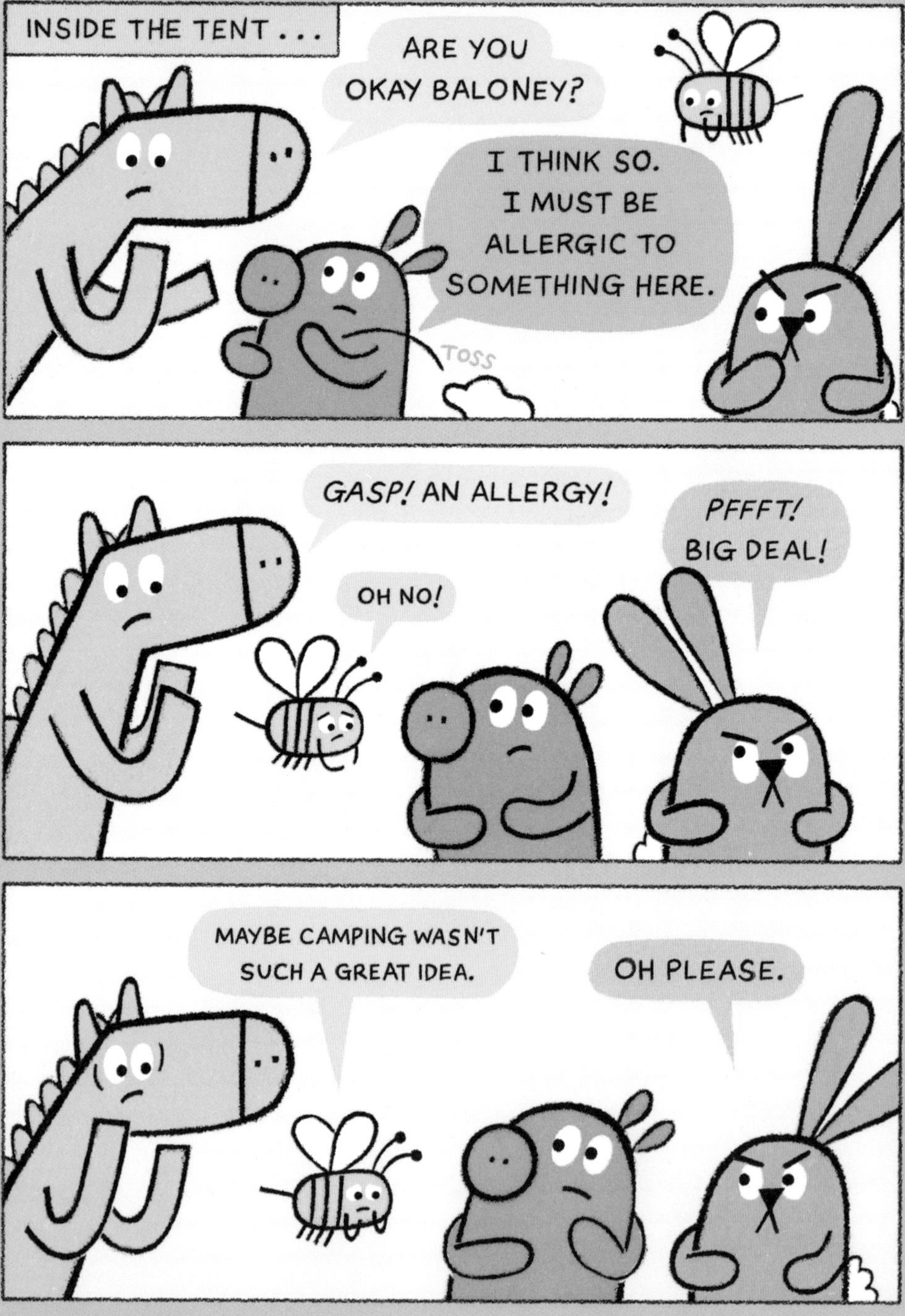
INSIDE THE TENT . . .
ARE YOU OKAY BALONEY?
I THINK SO. I MUST BE ALLERGIC TO SOMETHING HERE.
TOSS
GASP! AN ALLERGY!
OH NO!
PFFFT! BIG DEAL!
MAYBE CAMPING WASN'T SUCH A GREAT IDEA.
OH PLEASE.

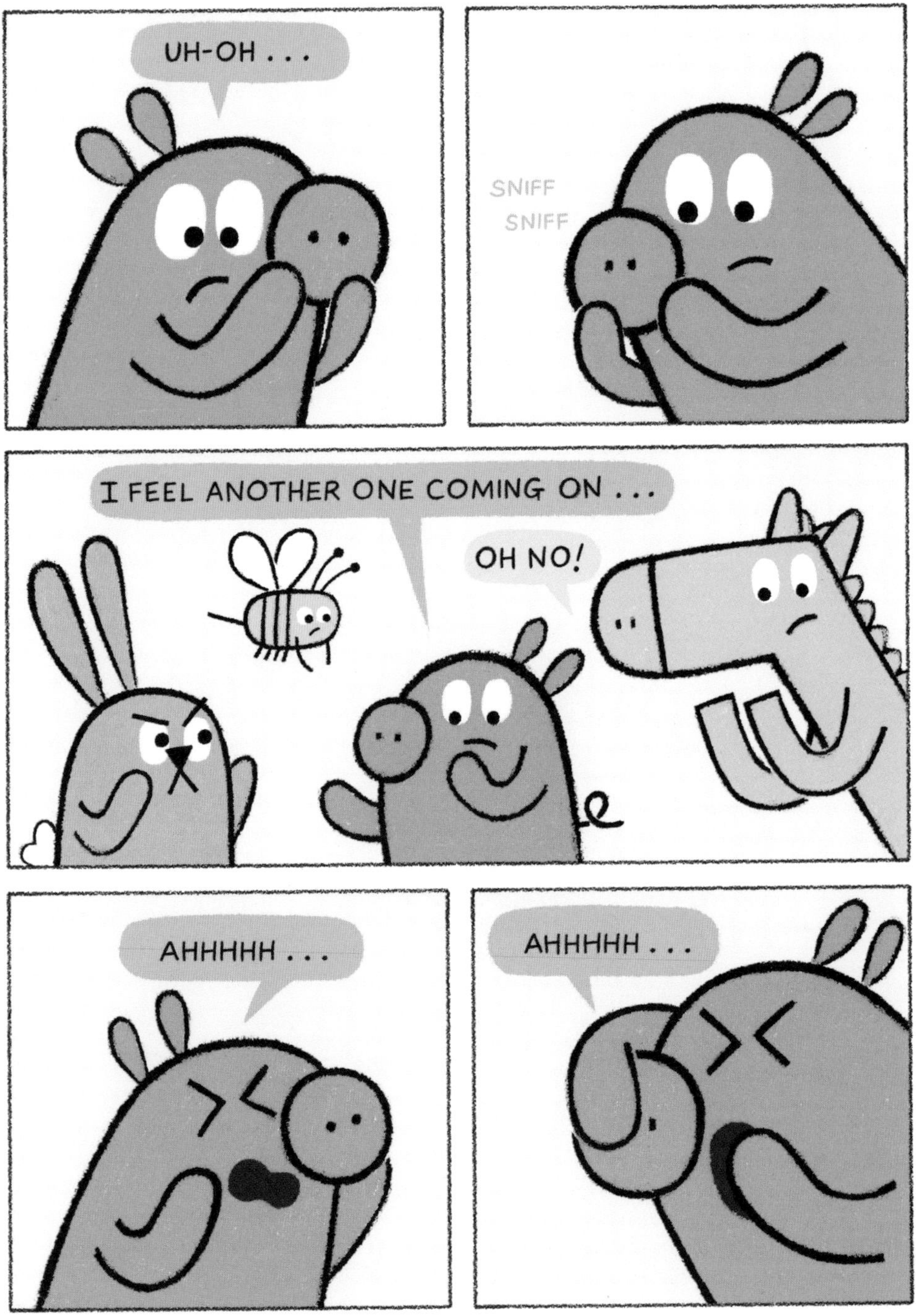
UH-OH . . .
SNIFF
SNIFF
I FEEL ANOTHER ONE COMING ON . . .
OH NO!
AHHHHH . . .
AHHHHH . . .

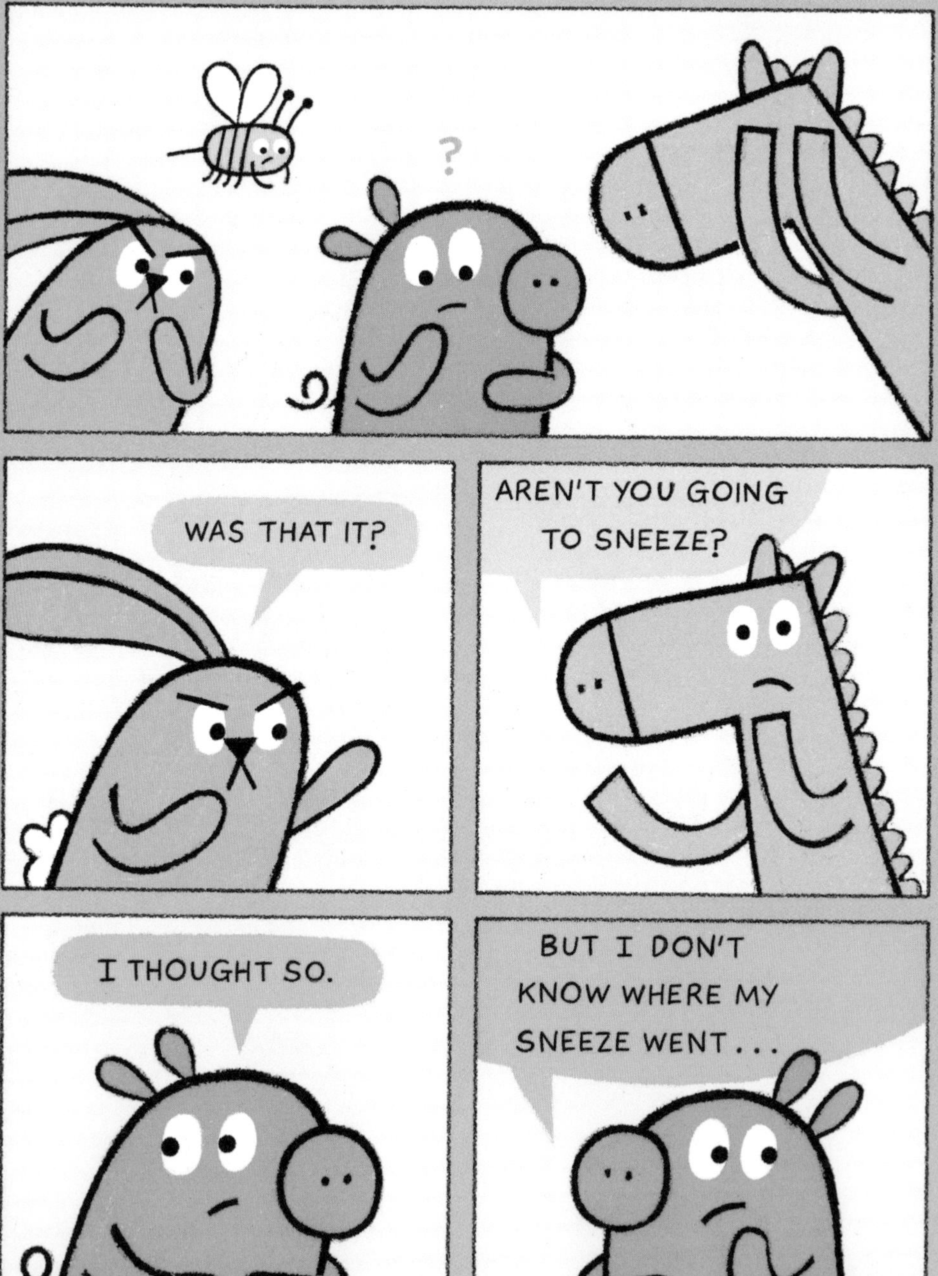
?
WAS THAT IT?
AREN'T YOU GOING TO SNEEZE?
I THOUGHT SO.
BUT I DON'T KNOW WHERE MY SNEEZE WENT . . .

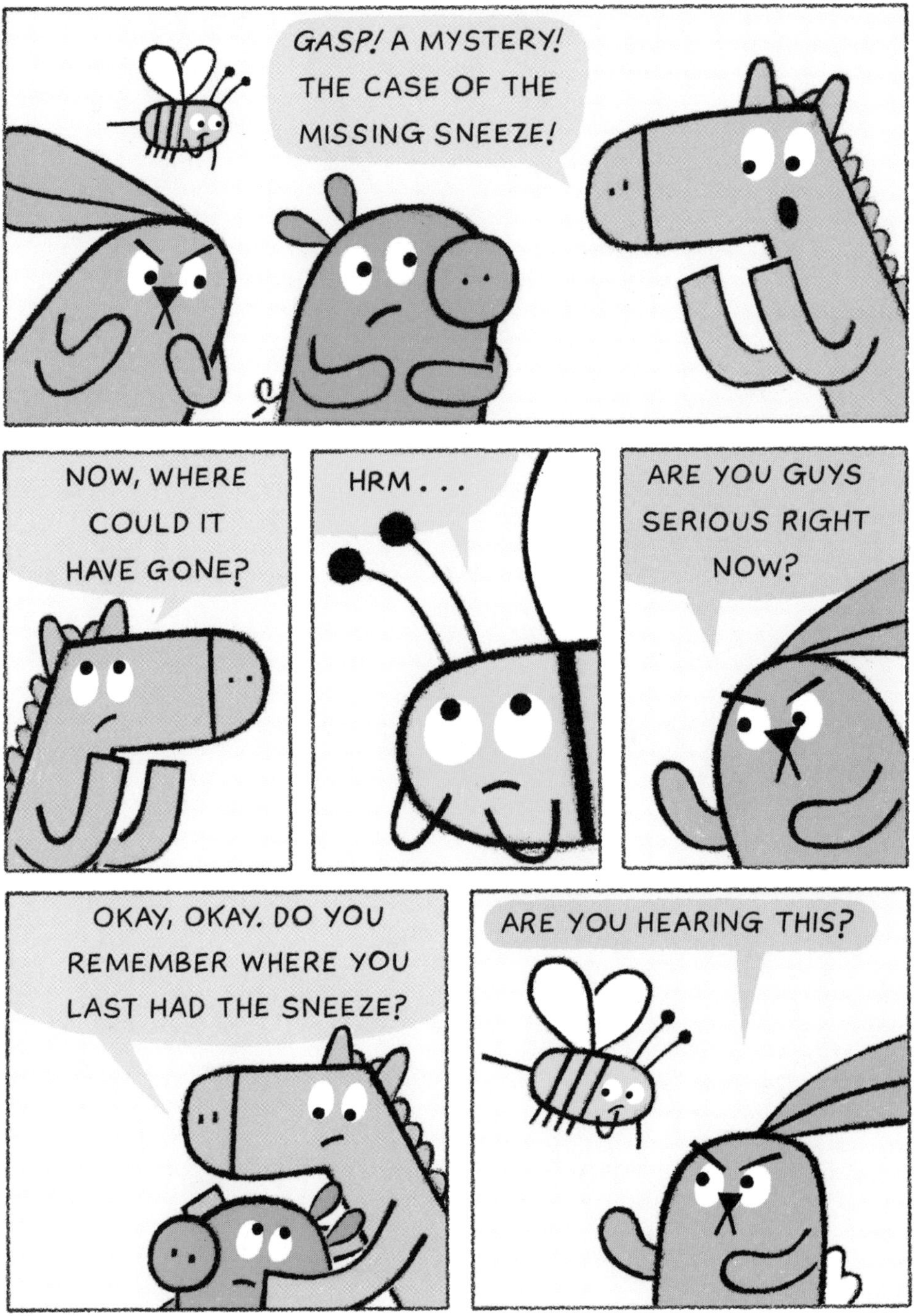
GASP! A MYSTERY! THE CASE OF THE MISSING SNEEZE!
NOW, WHERE COULD IT HAVE GONE?
HRM . . .
ARE YOU GUYS SERIOUS RIGHT NOW?
OKAY, OKAY. DO YOU REMEMBER WHERE YOU LAST HAD THE SNEEZE?
ARE YOU HEARING THIS?

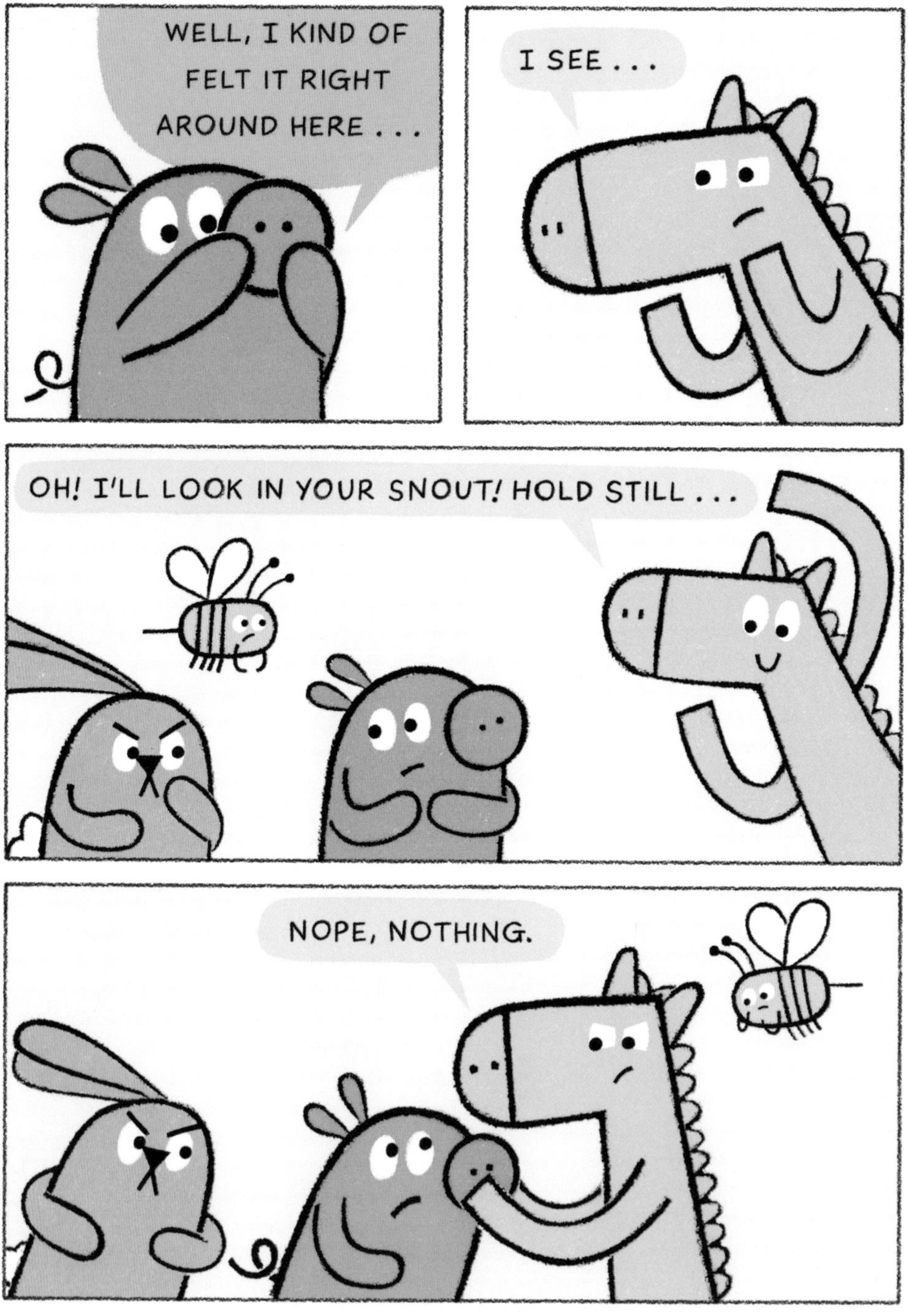
WELL, I KIND OF FELT IT RIGHT AROUND HERE . . .
I SEE . . .
OH! I'LL LOOK IN YOUR SNOUT! HOLD STILL . . .
NOPE, NOTHING.

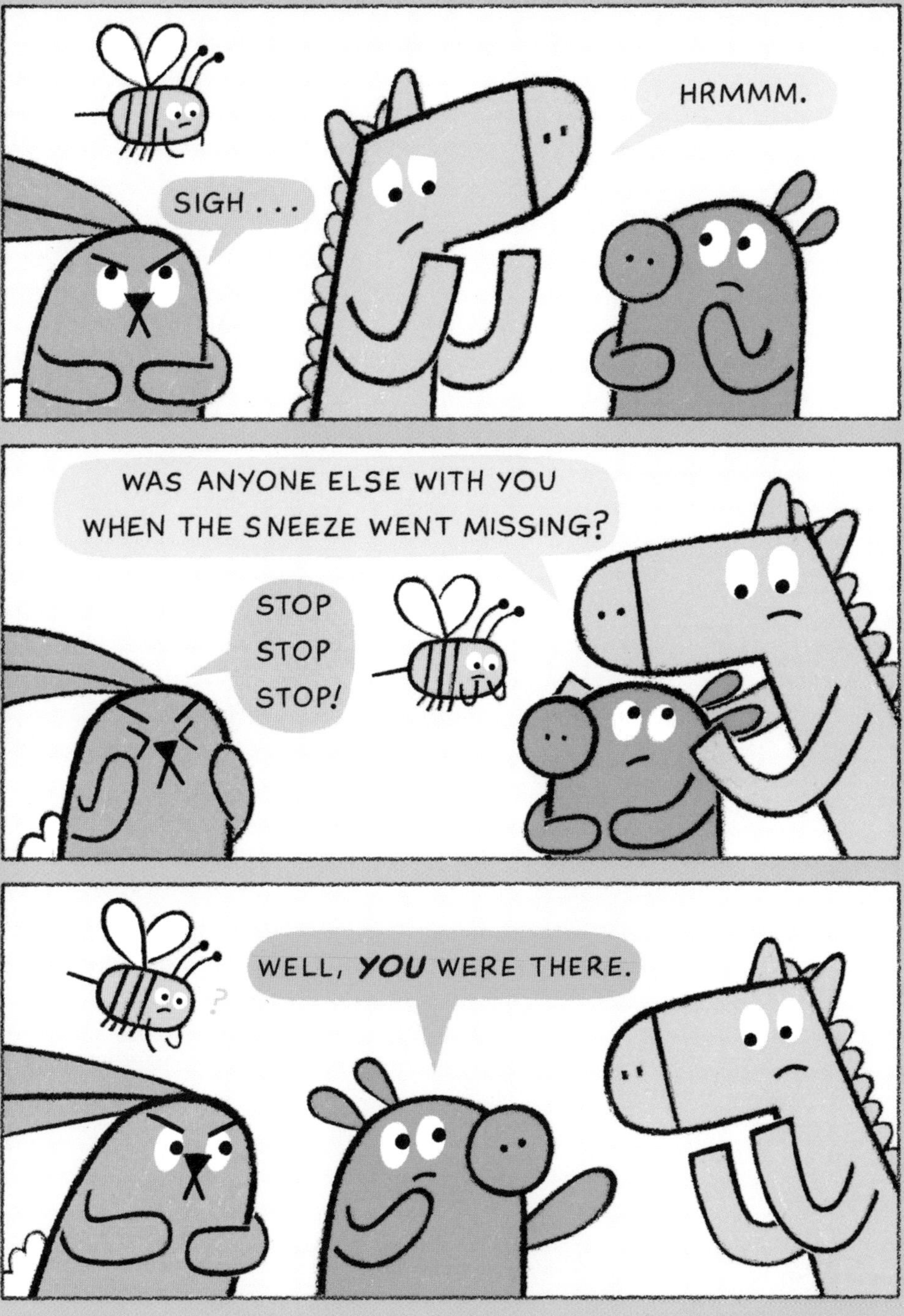
HRMMM.
SIGH . . .
WAS ANYONE ELSE WITH YOU WHEN THE SNEEZE WENT MISSING?
STOP STOP STOP!
WELL, ***YOU*** WERE THERE.

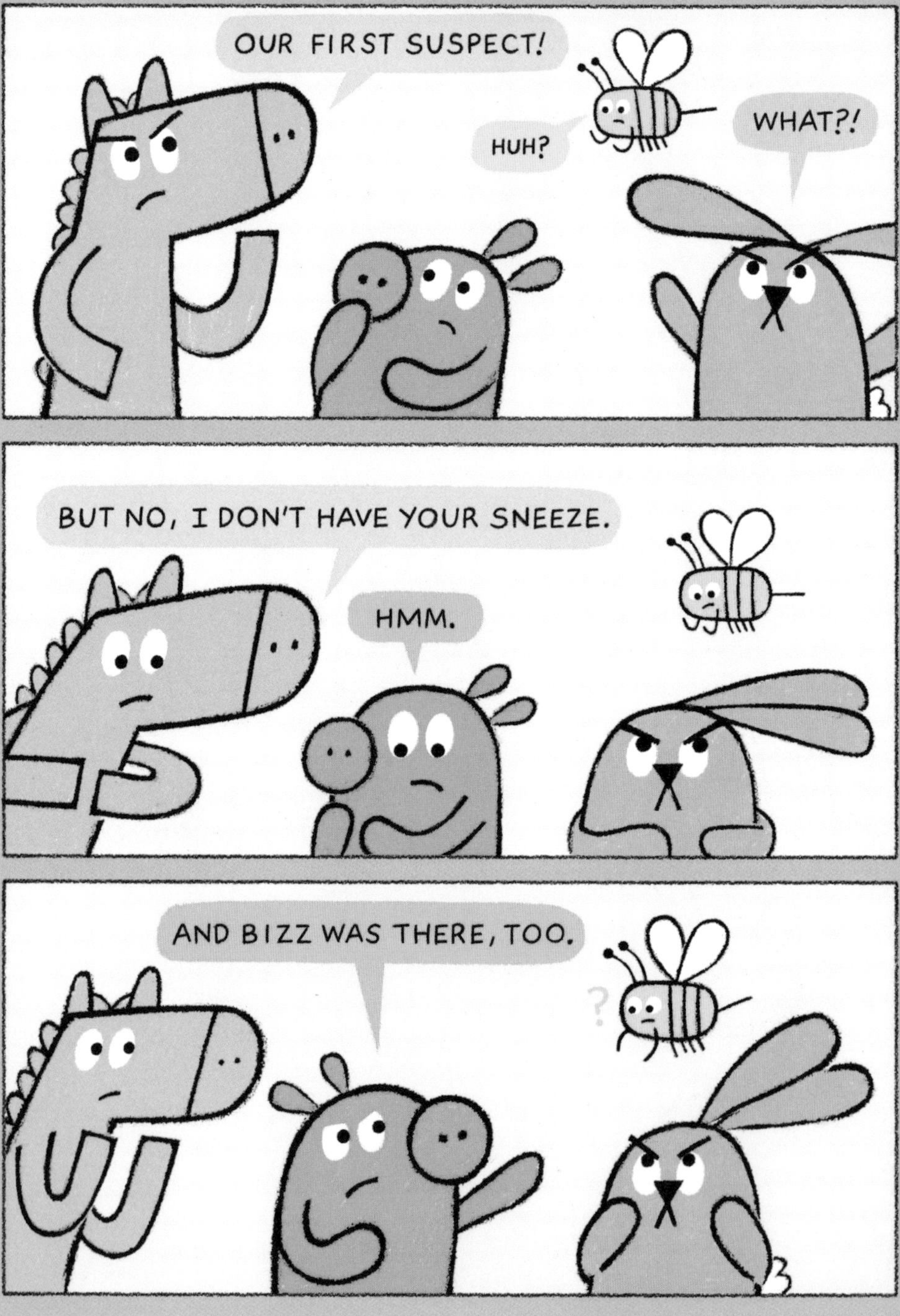
OUR FIRST SUSPECT!
HUH?
WHAT?!
BUT NO, I DON'T HAVE YOUR SNEEZE.
HMM.
AND BIZZ WAS THERE, TOO.
?

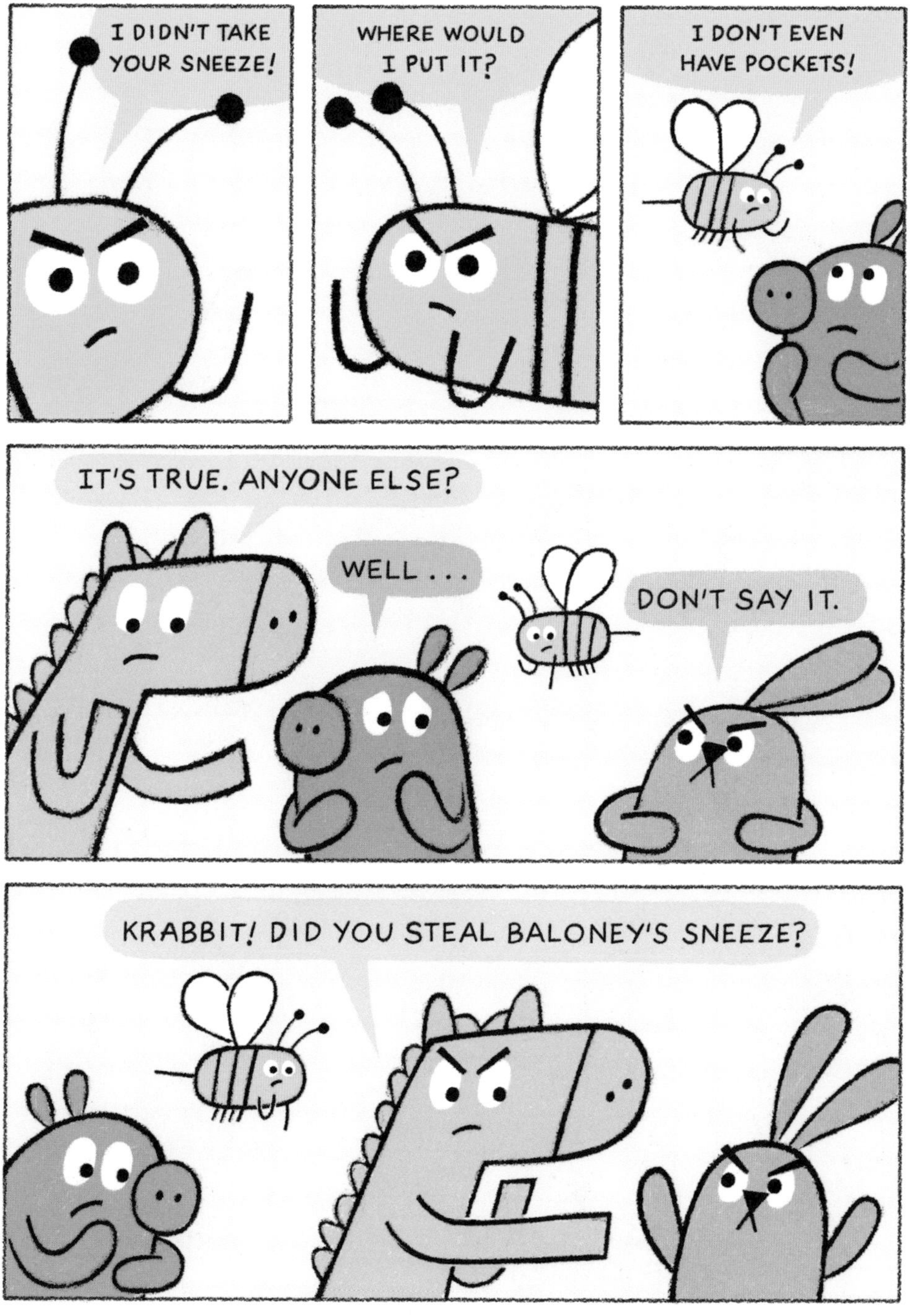

I DIDN'T TAKE YOUR SNEEZE!
WHERE WOULD I PUT IT?
I DON'T EVEN HAVE POCKETS!
IT'S TRUE. ANYONE ELSE?
WELL . . .
DON'T SAY IT.
KRABBIT! DID YOU STEAL BALONEY'S SNEEZE?

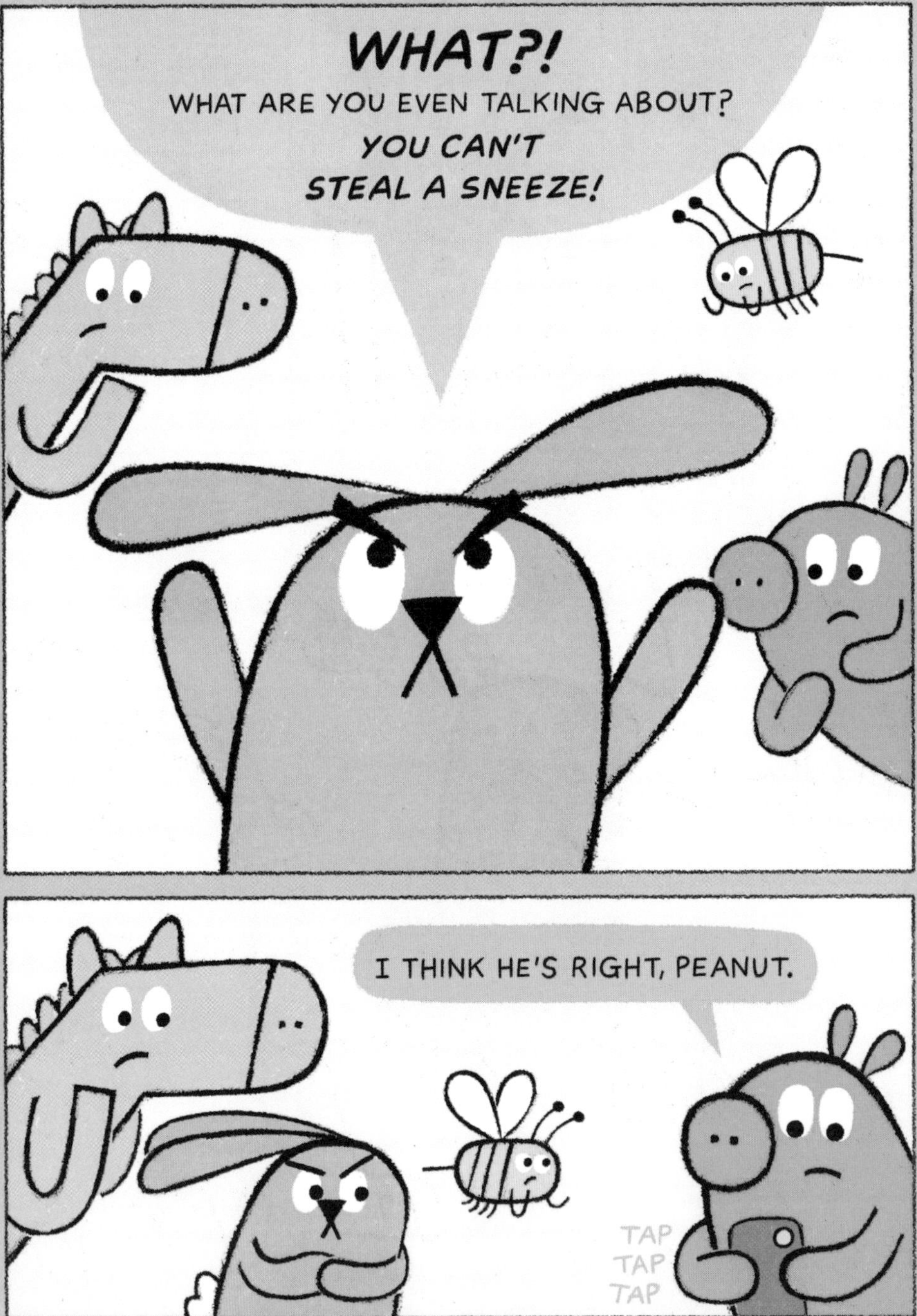
WHAT?!
WHAT ARE YOU EVEN TALKING ABOUT?
YOU CAN'T STEAL A SNEEZE!
I THINK HE'S RIGHT, PEANUT.
TAP TAP TAP

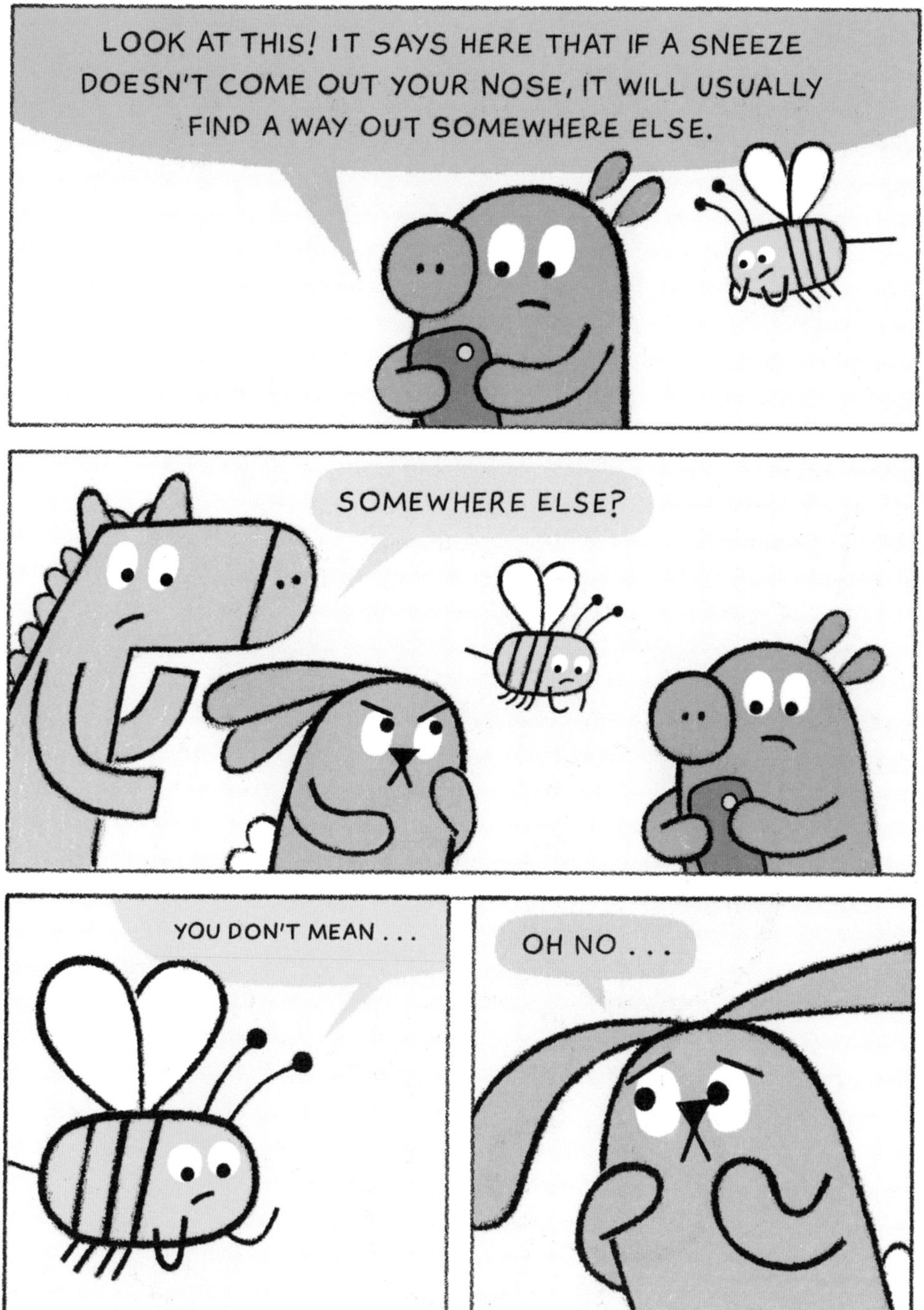
LOOK AT THIS! IT SAYS HERE THAT IF A SNEEZE DOESN'T COME OUT YOUR NOSE, IT WILL USUALLY FIND A WAY OUT SOMEWHERE ELSE.
SOMEWHERE ELSE?
YOU DON'T MEAN . . .
OH NO . . .

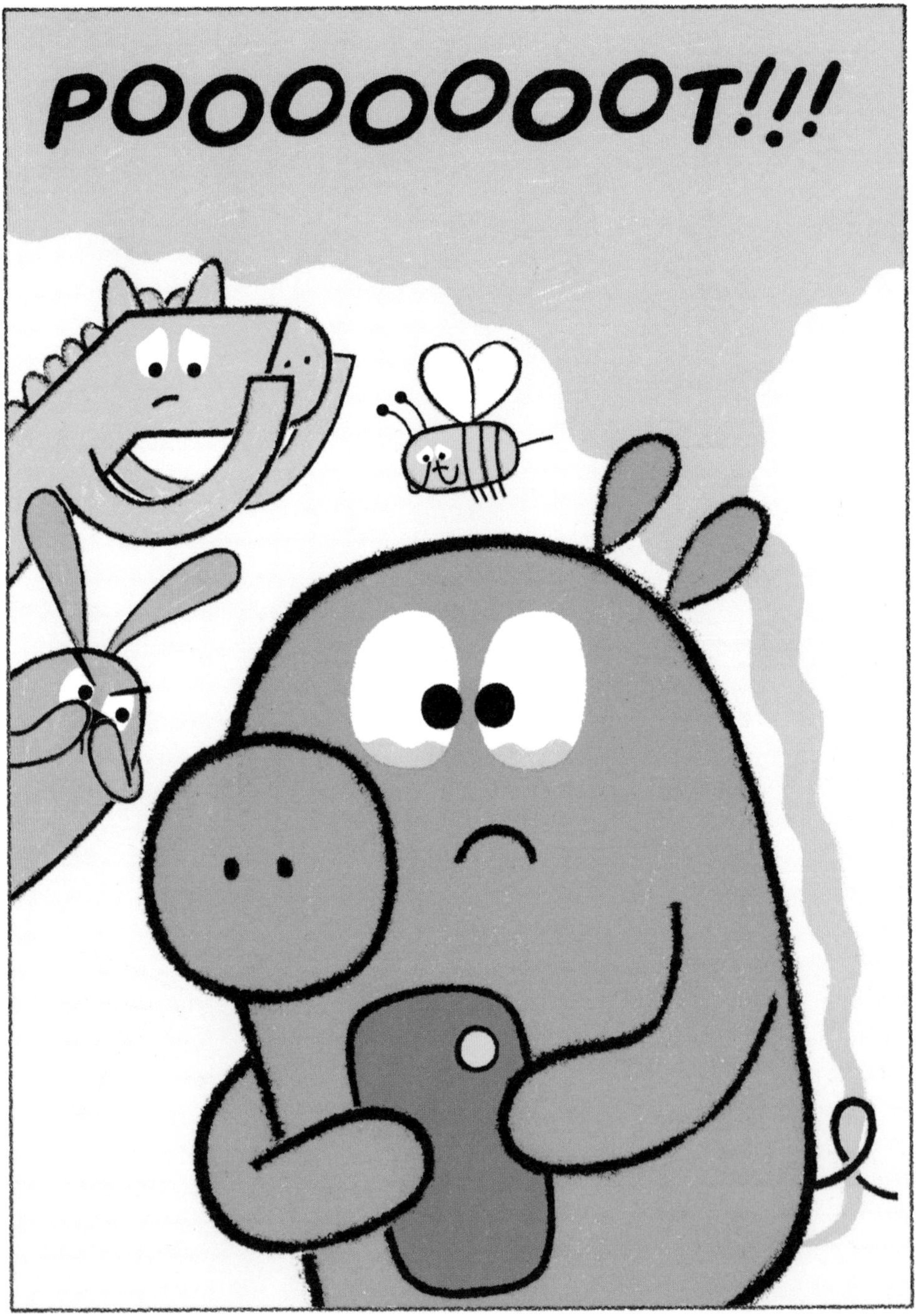
POOOOOOOT!!!

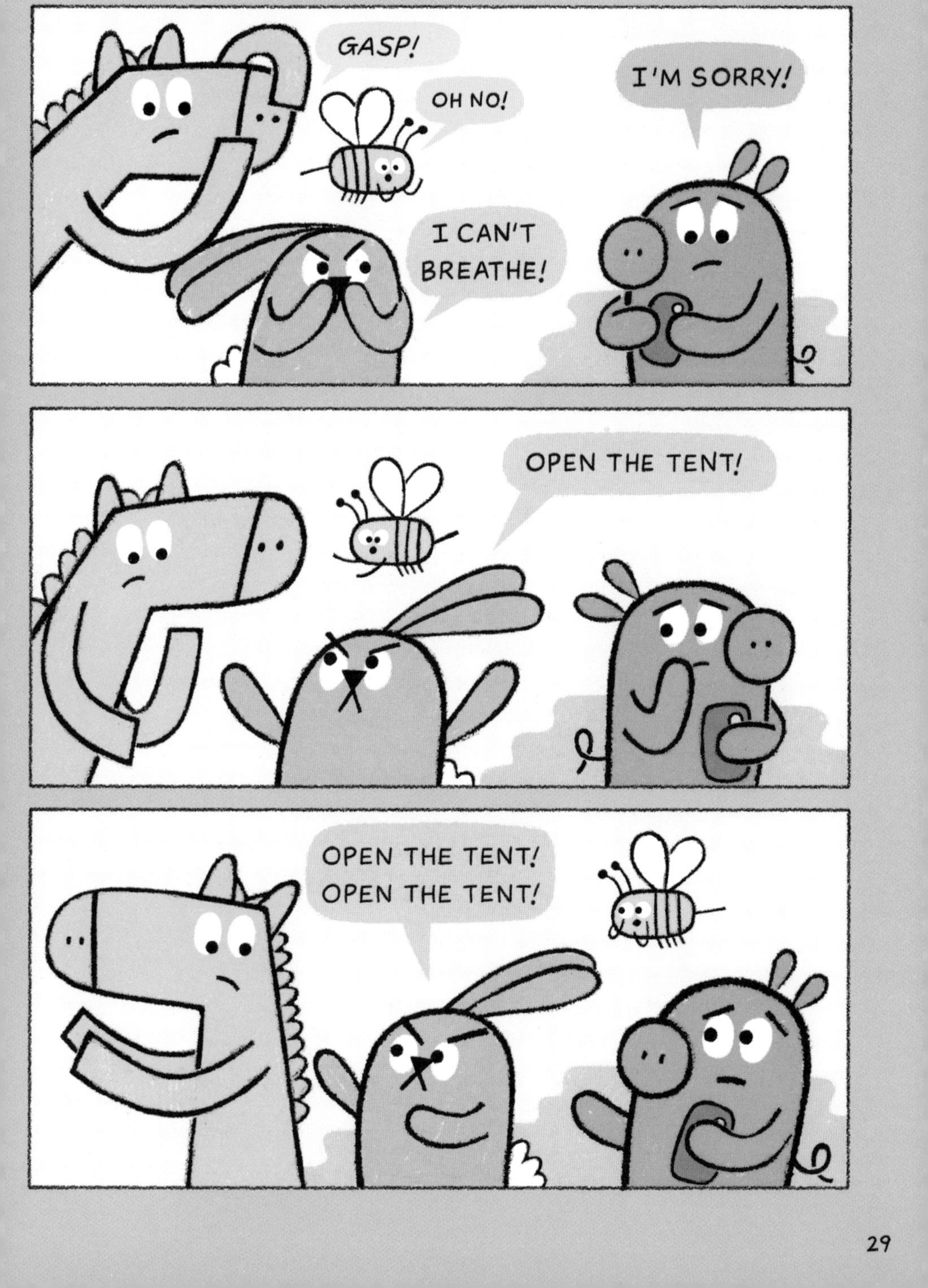
GASP!
OH NO!
I'M SORRY!
I CAN'T BREATHE!
OPEN THE TENT!
OPEN THE TENT! OPEN THE TENT!

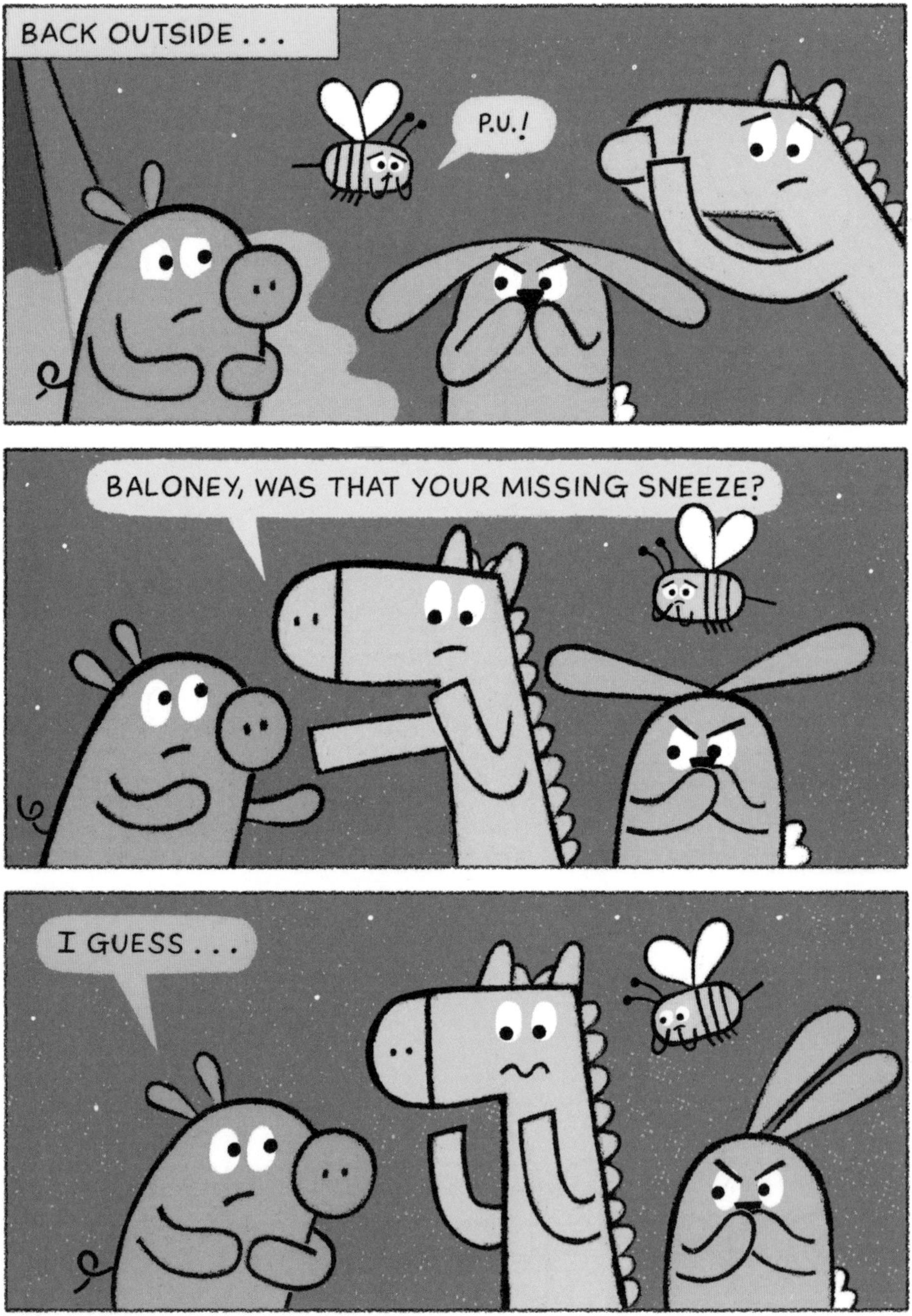
BACK OUTSIDE . . .
P.U.!
BALONEY, WAS THAT YOUR MISSING SNEEZE?
I GUESS . . .

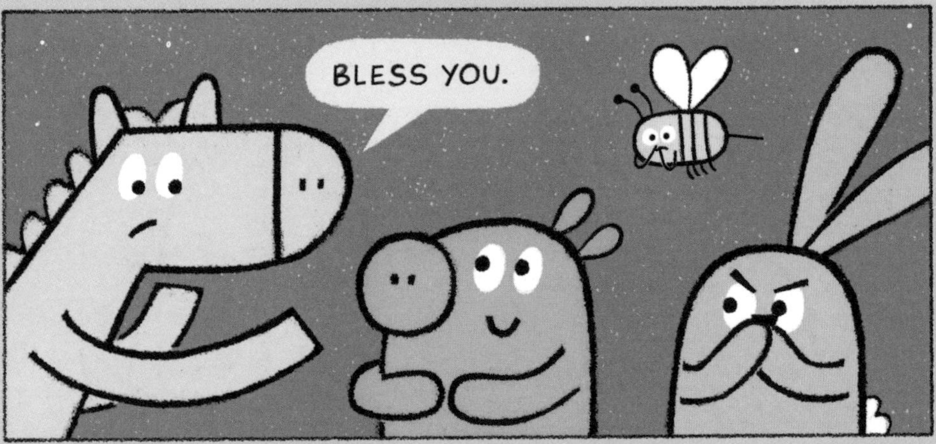
BLESS YOU.

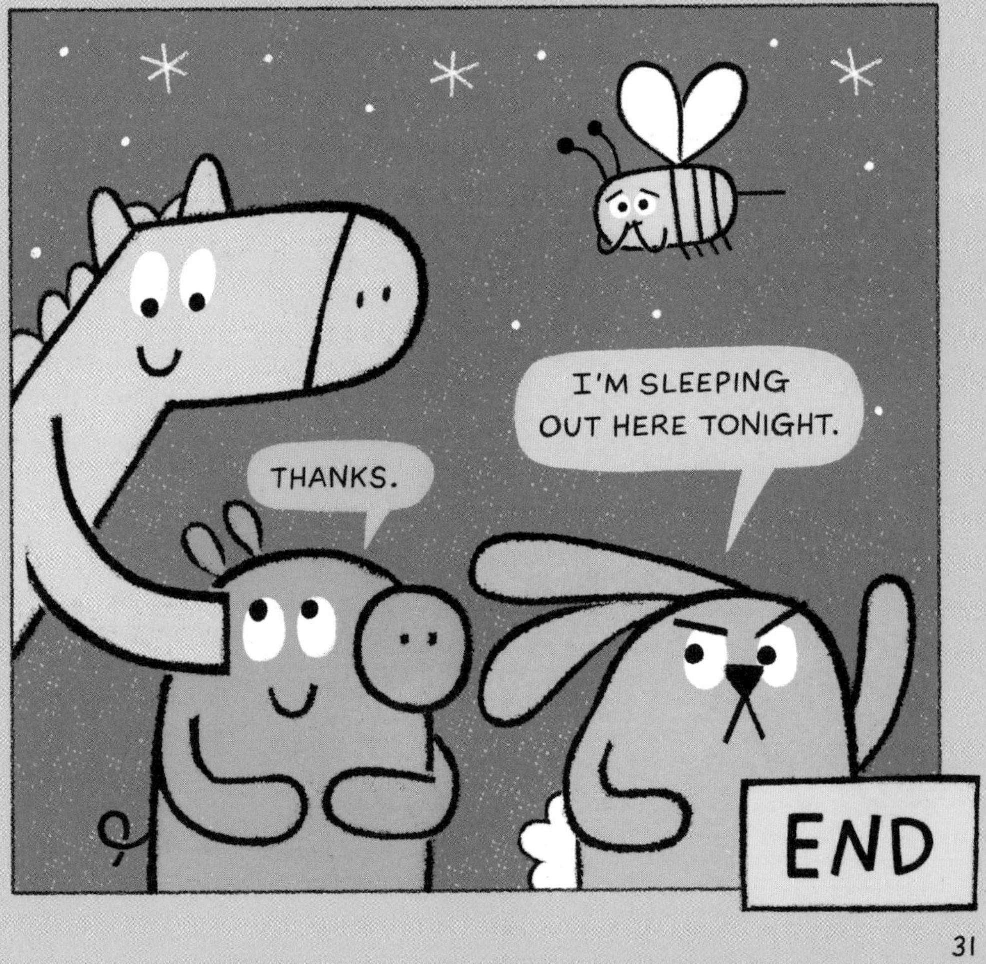
I'M SLEEPING
OUT HERE TONIGHT.
THANKS.
END

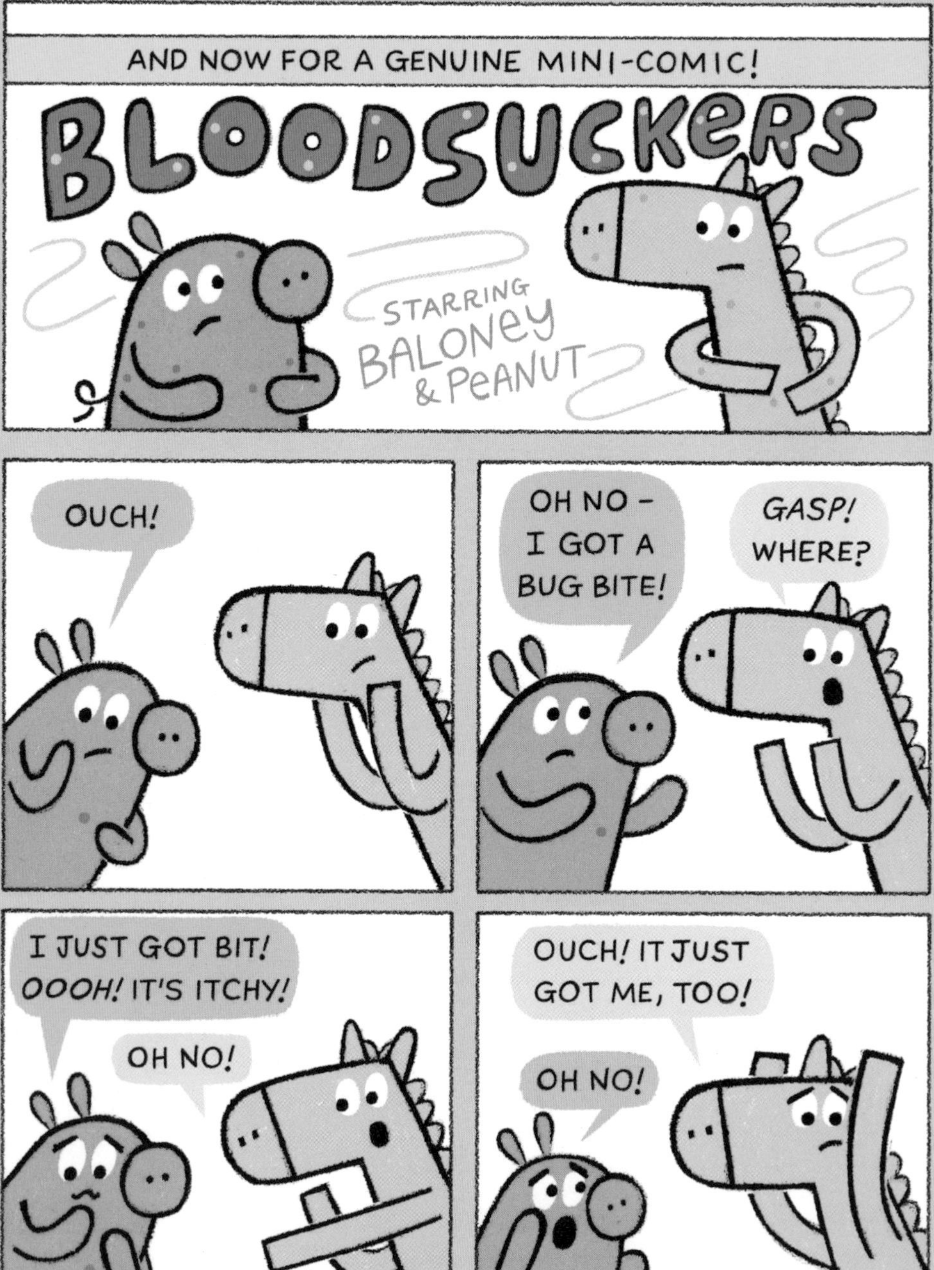
AND NOW FOR A GENUINE MINI-COMIC!
BLOODSUCKERS
STARRING BALONEY & PEANUT
OUCH!
OH NO - I GOT A BUG BITE!
GASP! WHERE?
I JUST GOT BIT! OOOH! IT'S ITCHY!
OH NO!
OUCH! IT JUST GOT ME, TOO!
OH NO!

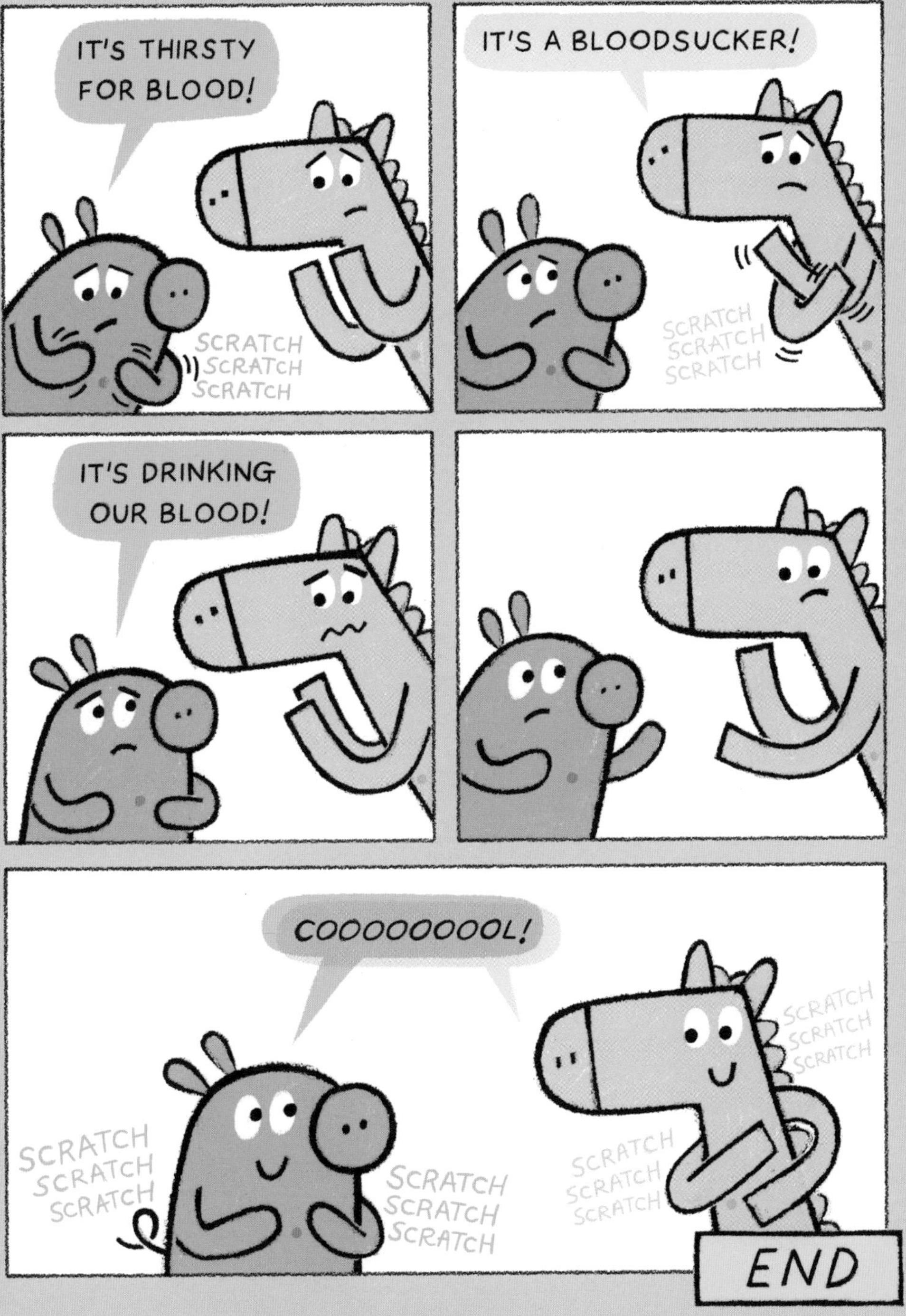
IT'S THIRSTY FOR BLOOD!
SCRATCH SCRATCH SCRATCH
IT'S A BLOODSUCKER!
SCRATCH SCRATCH SCRATCH
IT'S DRINKING OUR BLOOD!
COOOOOOOOL!
SCRATCH SCRATCH SCRATCH
SCRATCH SCRATCH SCRATCH
SCRATCH SCRATCH SCRATCH
SCRATCH SCRATCH SCRATCH
END

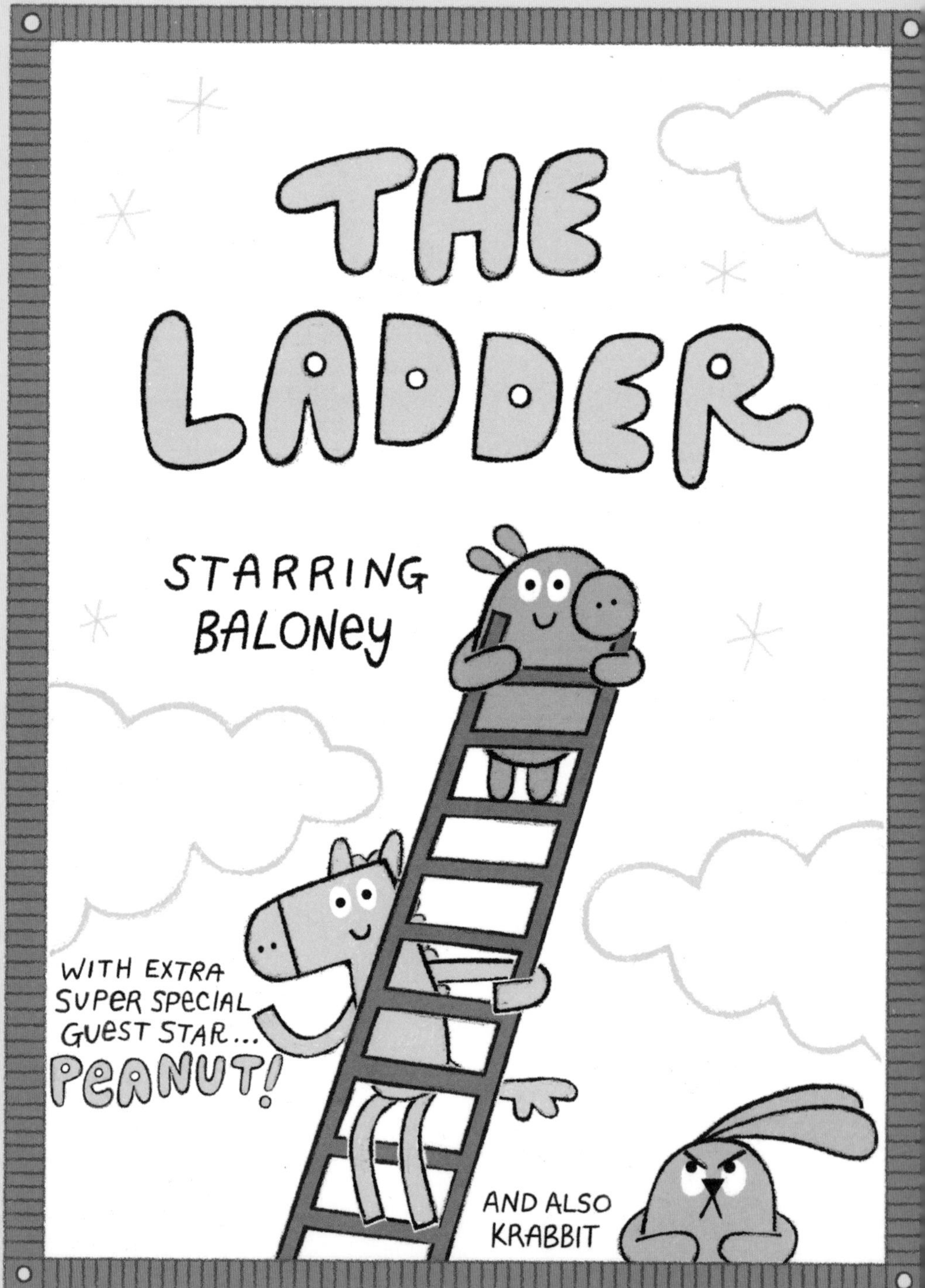
THE LADDER
STARRING BALONEY
WITH EXTRA SUPER SPECIAL GUEST STAR... PEANUT!
AND ALSO KRABBIT

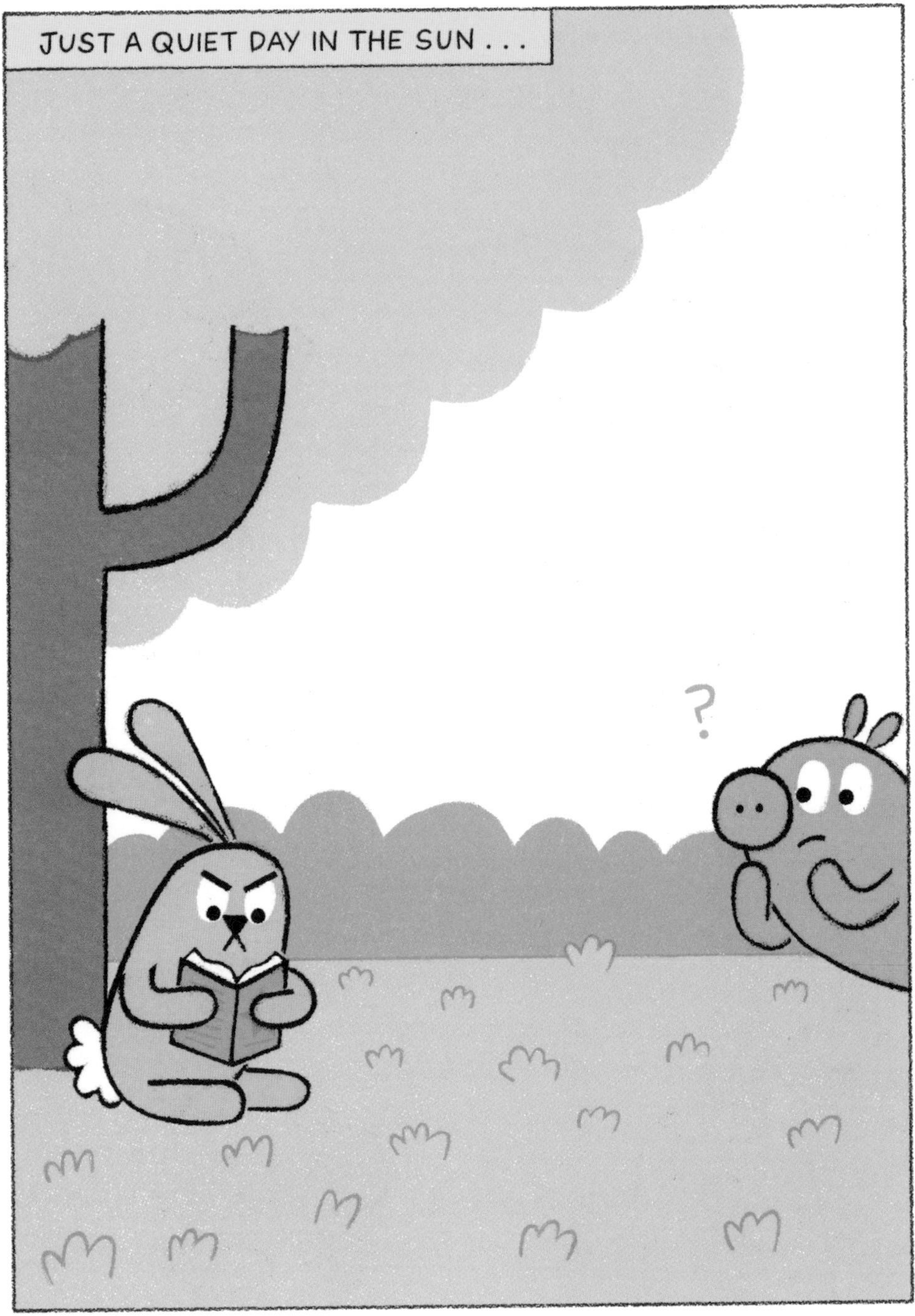
JUST A QUIET DAY IN THE SUN . . .
?

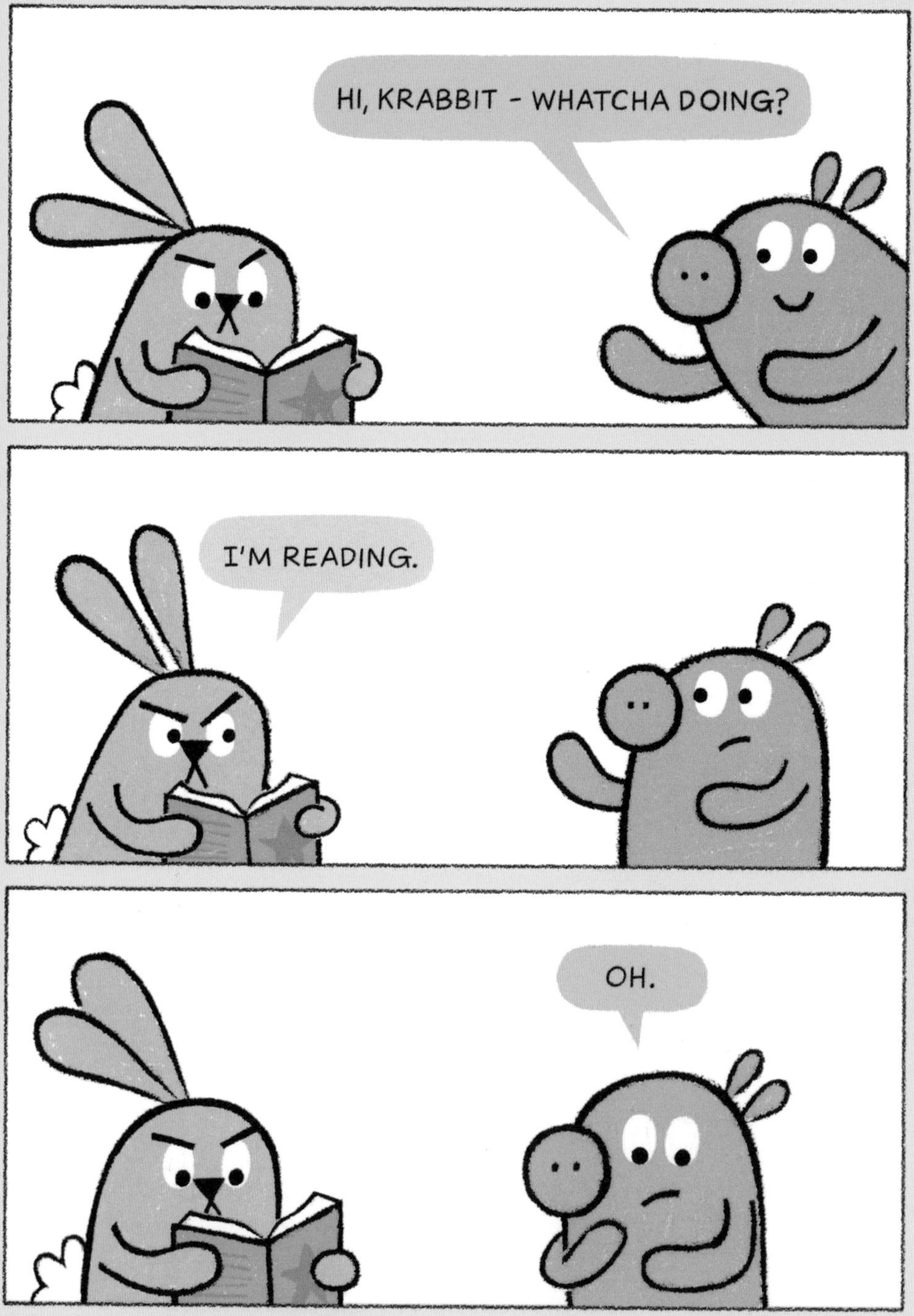
HI, KRABBIT - WHATCHA DOING?
I'M READING.
OH.

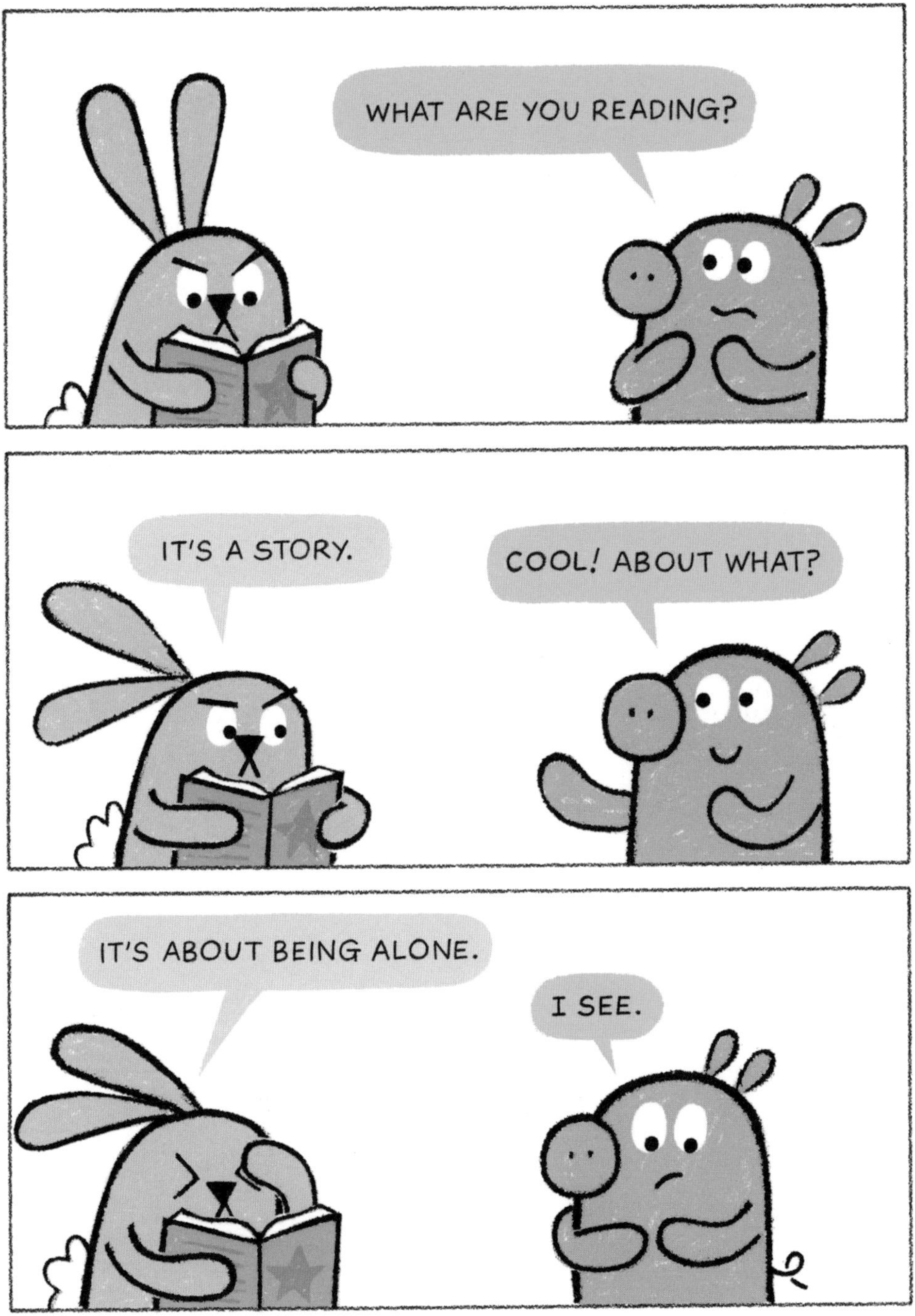
WHAT ARE YOU READING?
IT'S A STORY.
COOL! ABOUT WHAT?
IT'S ABOUT BEING ALONE.
I SEE.

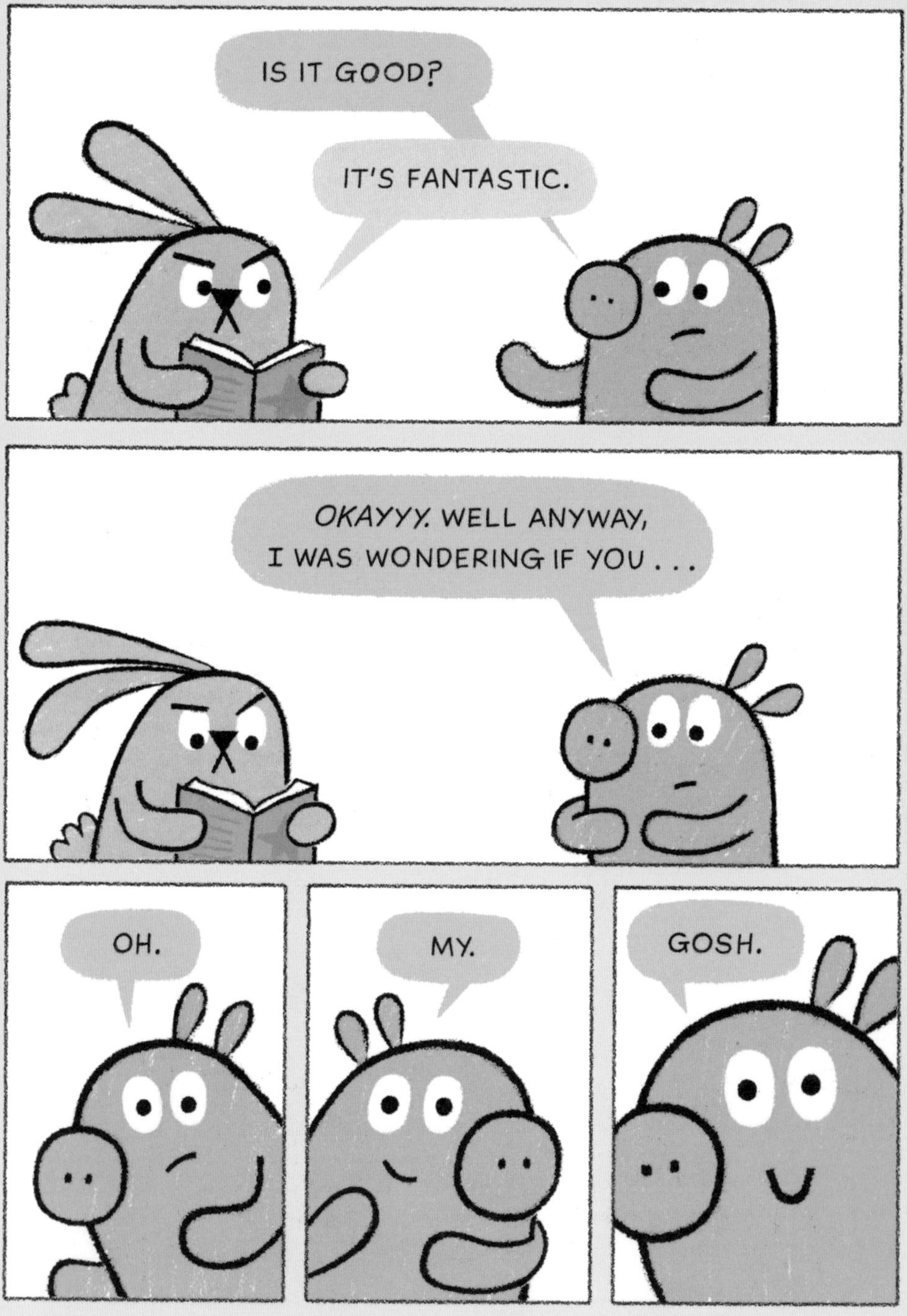
IS IT GOOD?
IT'S FANTASTIC.
OKAYYY. WELL ANYWAY, I WAS WONDERING IF YOU . . .
OH.
MY.
GOSH.

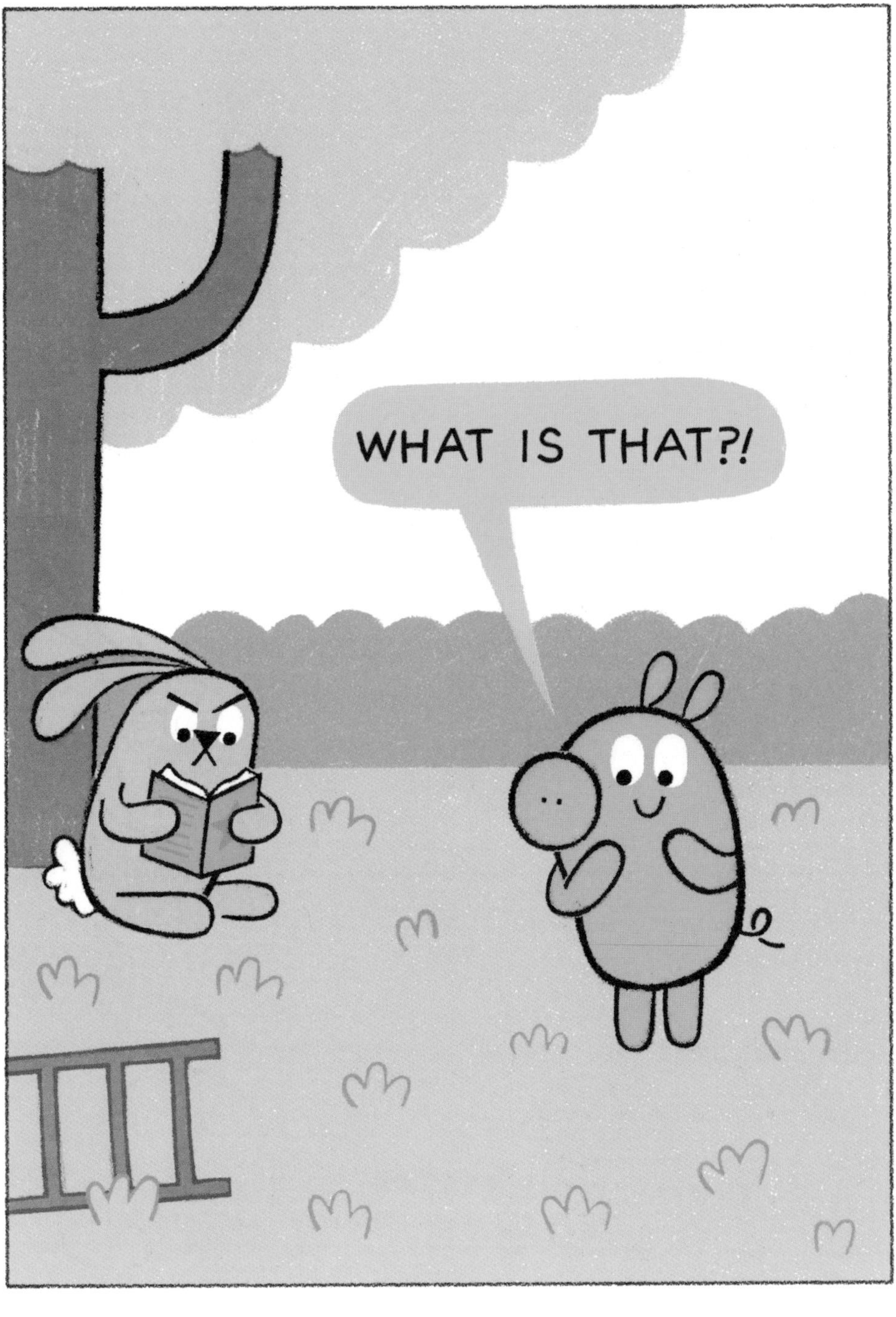
WHAT IS THAT?!

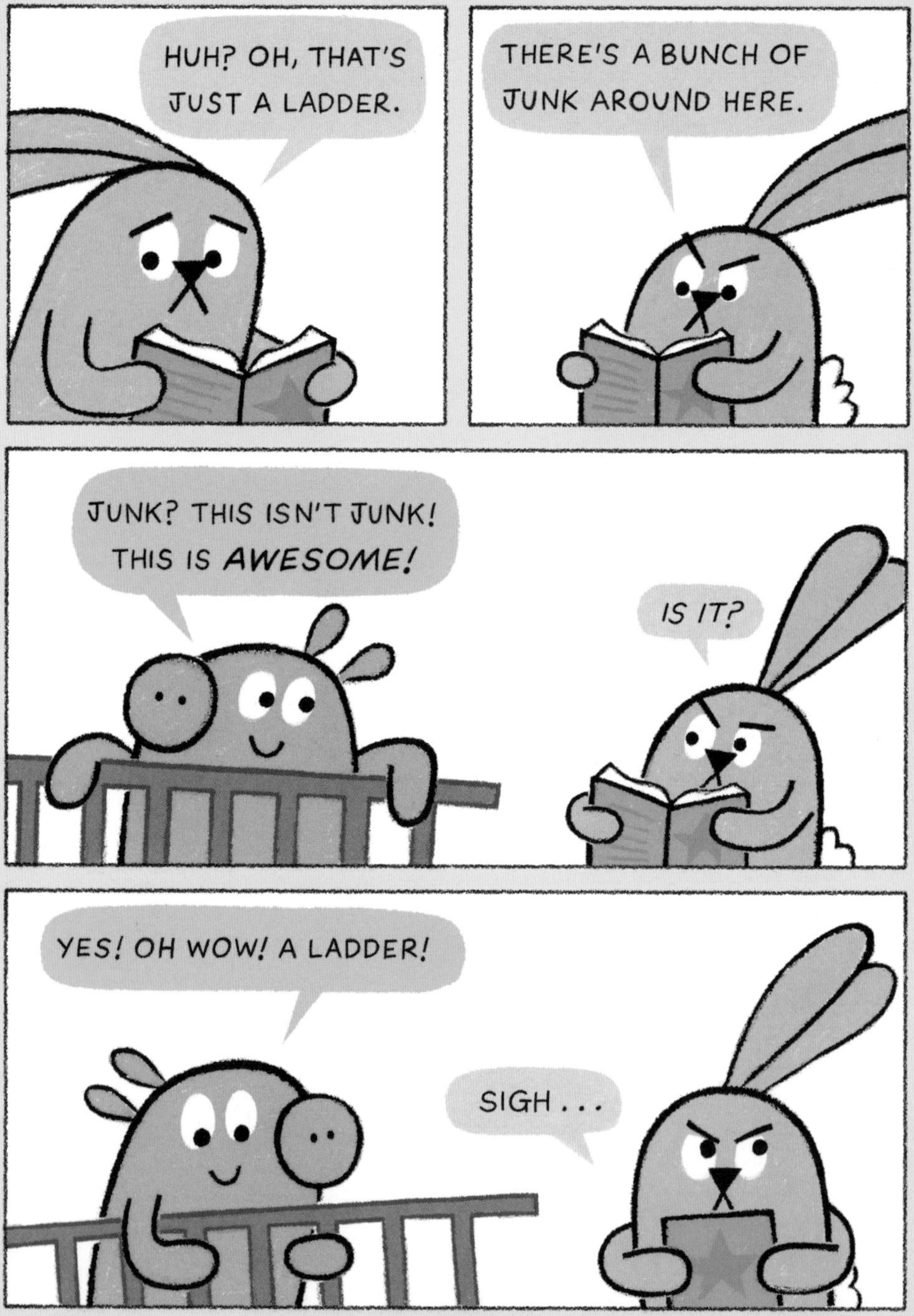
HUH? OH, THAT'S JUST A LADDER.
THERE'S A BUNCH OF JUNK AROUND HERE.
JUNK? THIS ISN'T JUNK! THIS IS *AWESOME!*
IS IT?
YES! OH WOW! A LADDER!
SIGH . . .

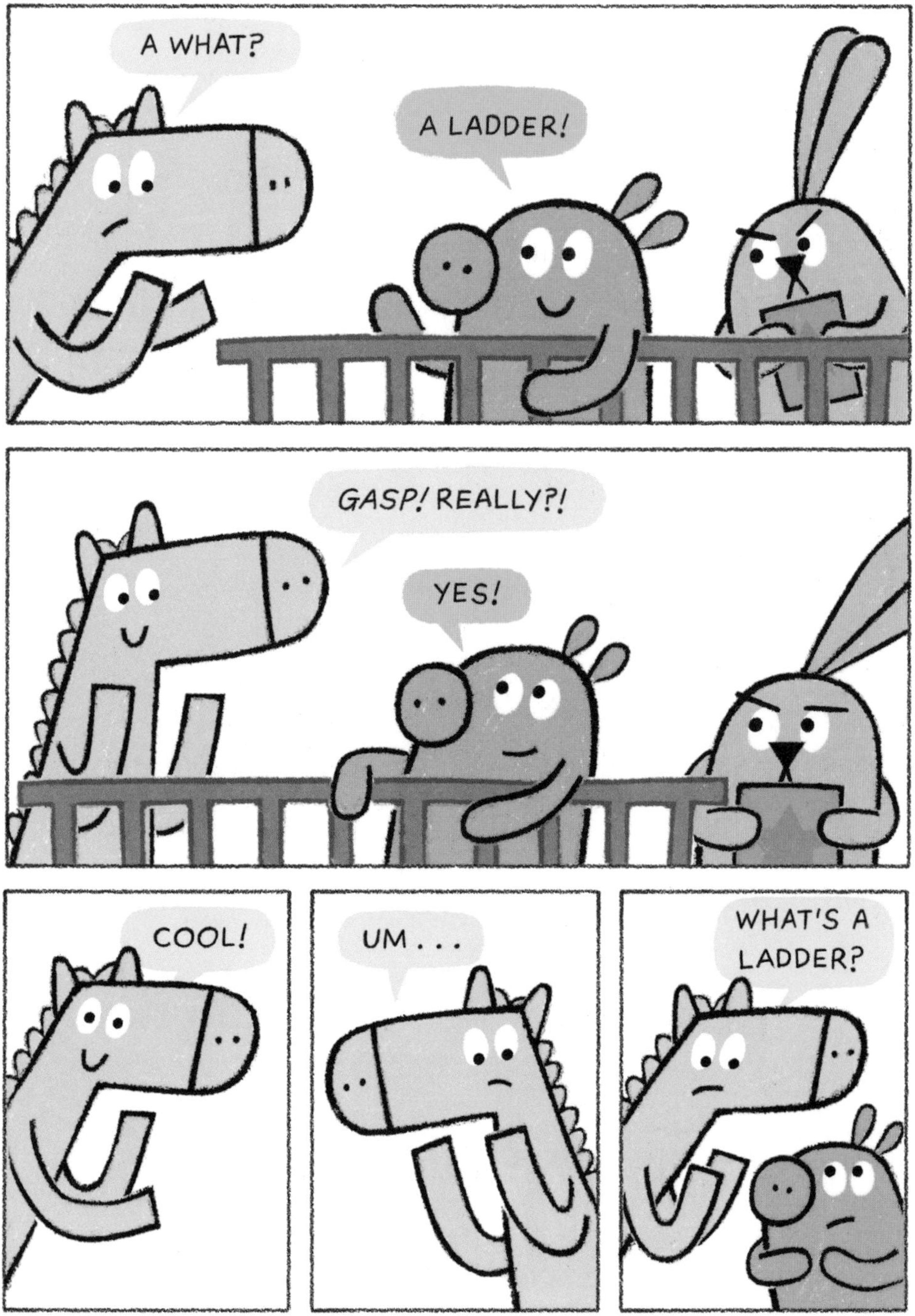
A WHAT?
A LADDER!
GASP! REALLY?!
YES!
COOL!
UM . . .
WHAT'S A LADDER?

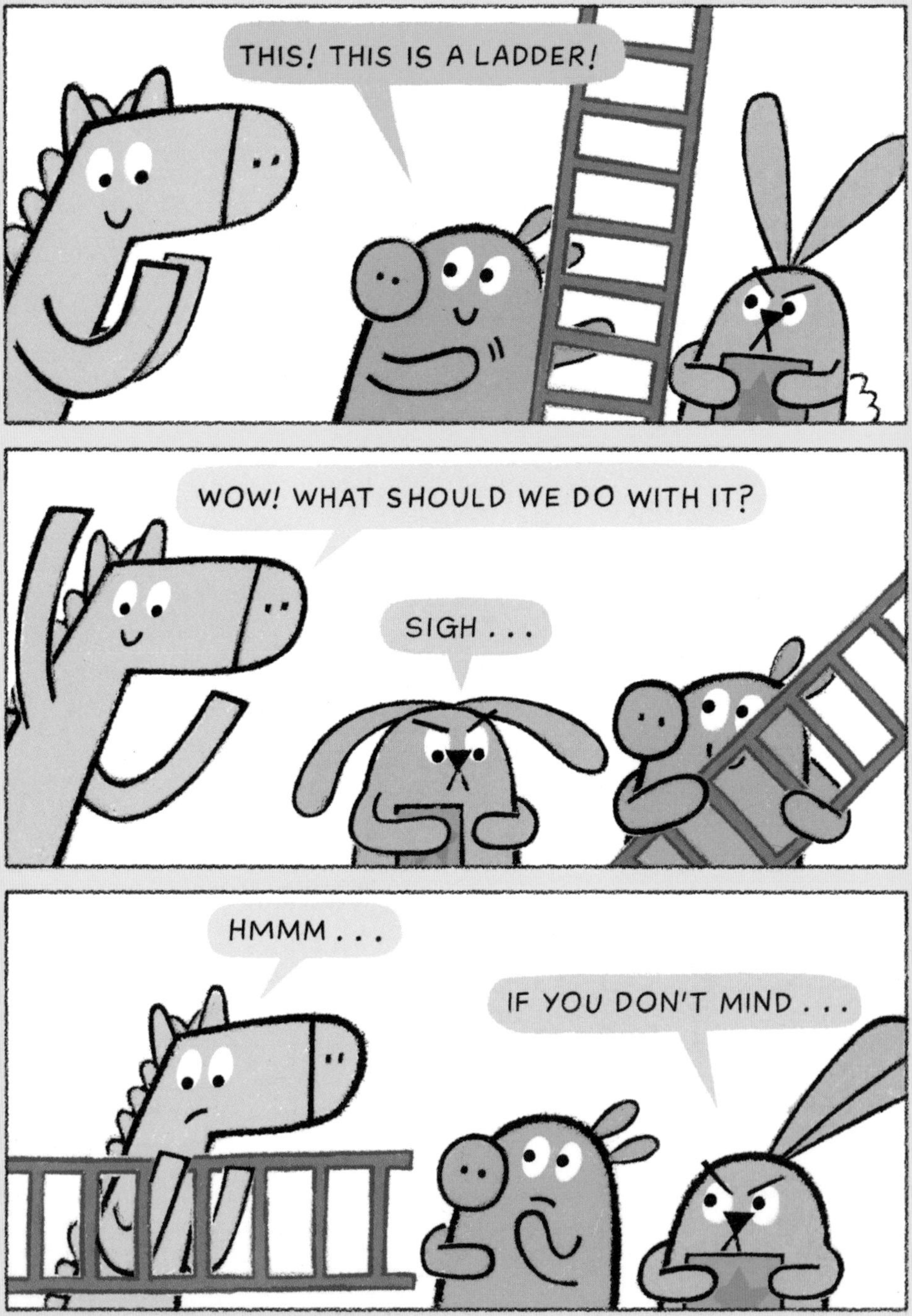
THIS! THIS IS A LADDER!
WOW! WHAT SHOULD WE DO WITH IT?
SIGH . . .
HMMM . . .
IF YOU DON'T MIND . . .

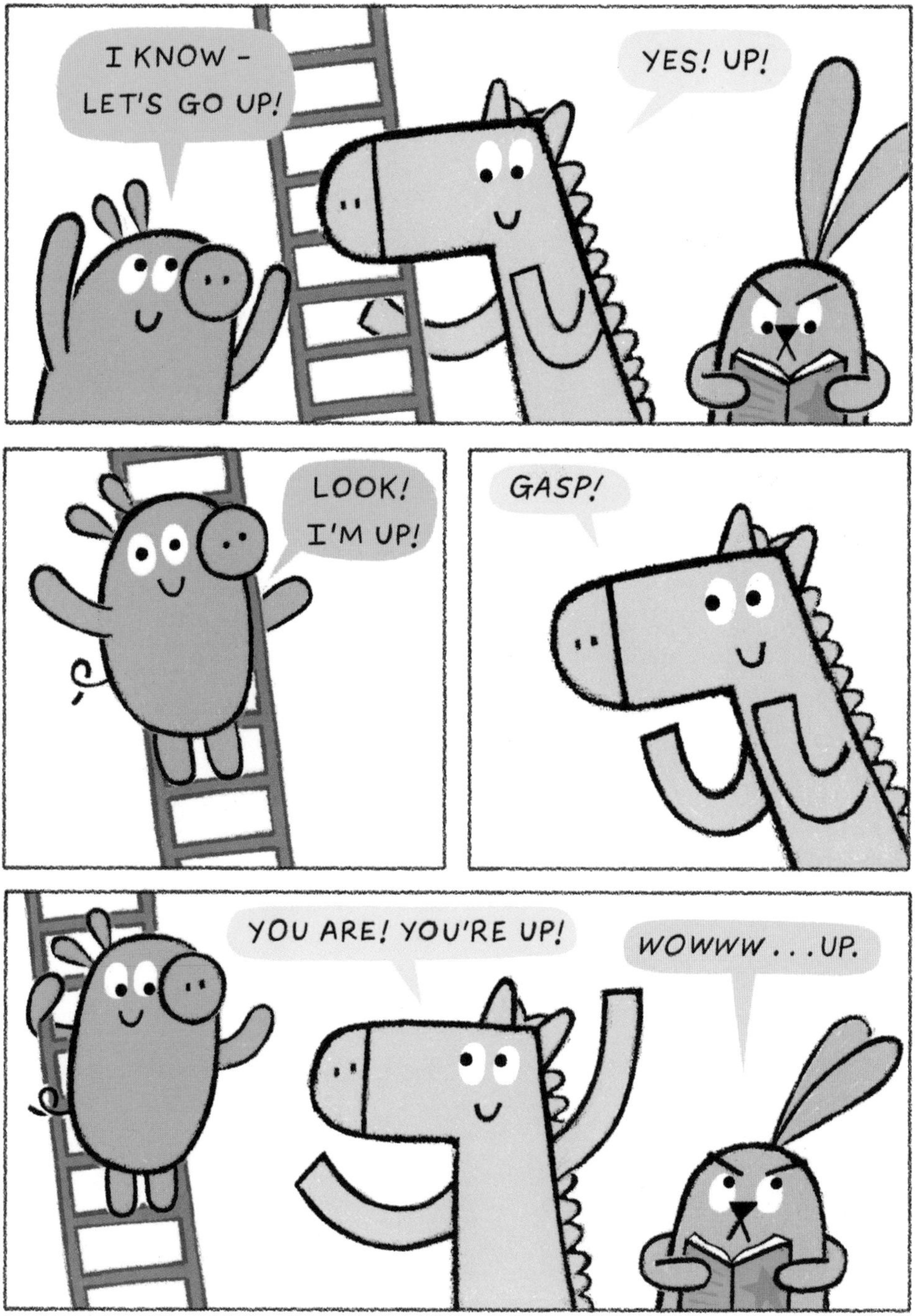
I KNOW - LET'S GO UP!
YES! UP!
LOOK! I'M UP!
GASP!
YOU ARE! YOU'RE UP!
WOWWW . . . UP.

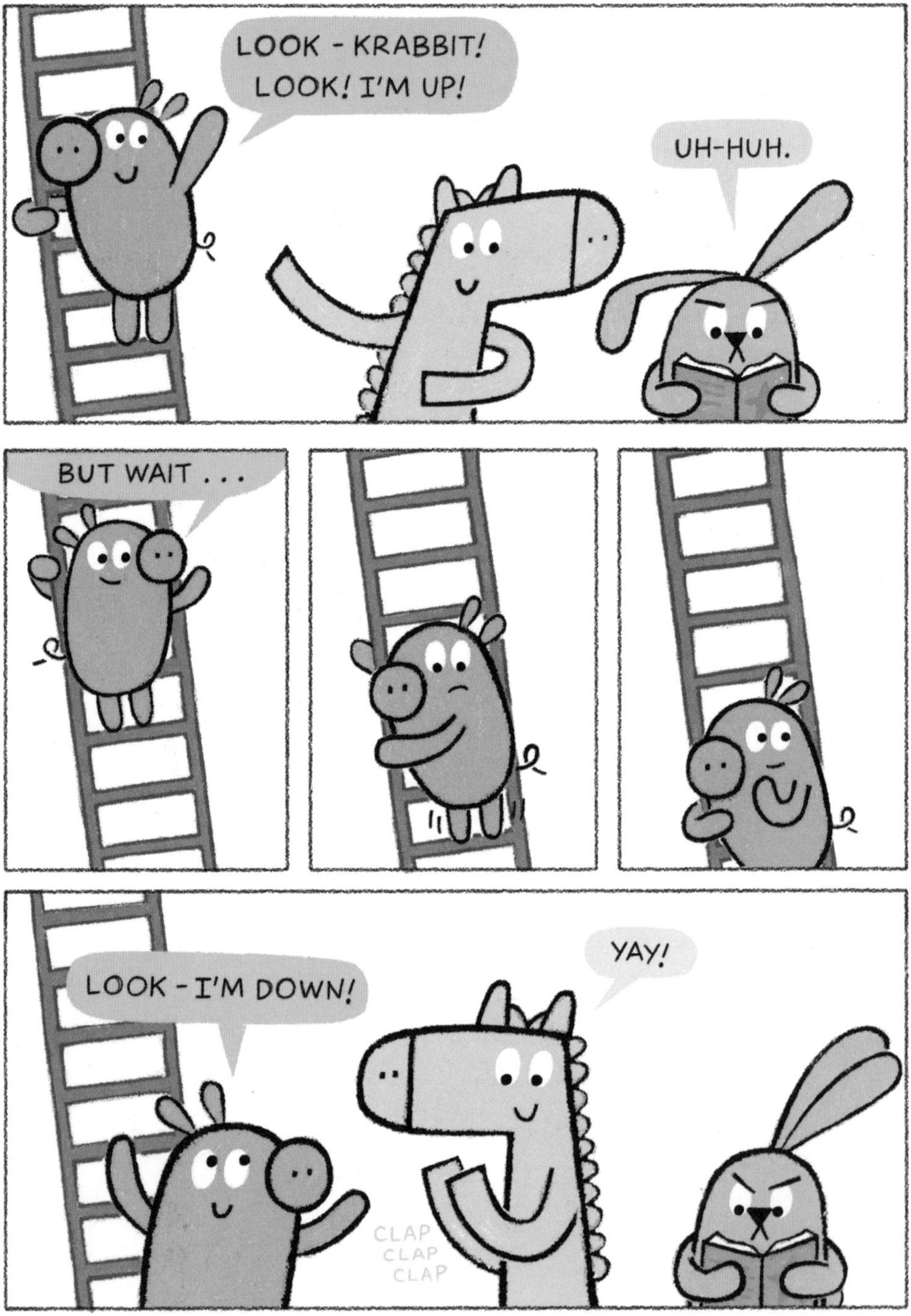
LOOK - KRABBIT! LOOK! I'M UP!
UH-HUH.
BUT WAIT . . .
LOOK - I'M DOWN!
YAY!
CLAP CLAP CLAP

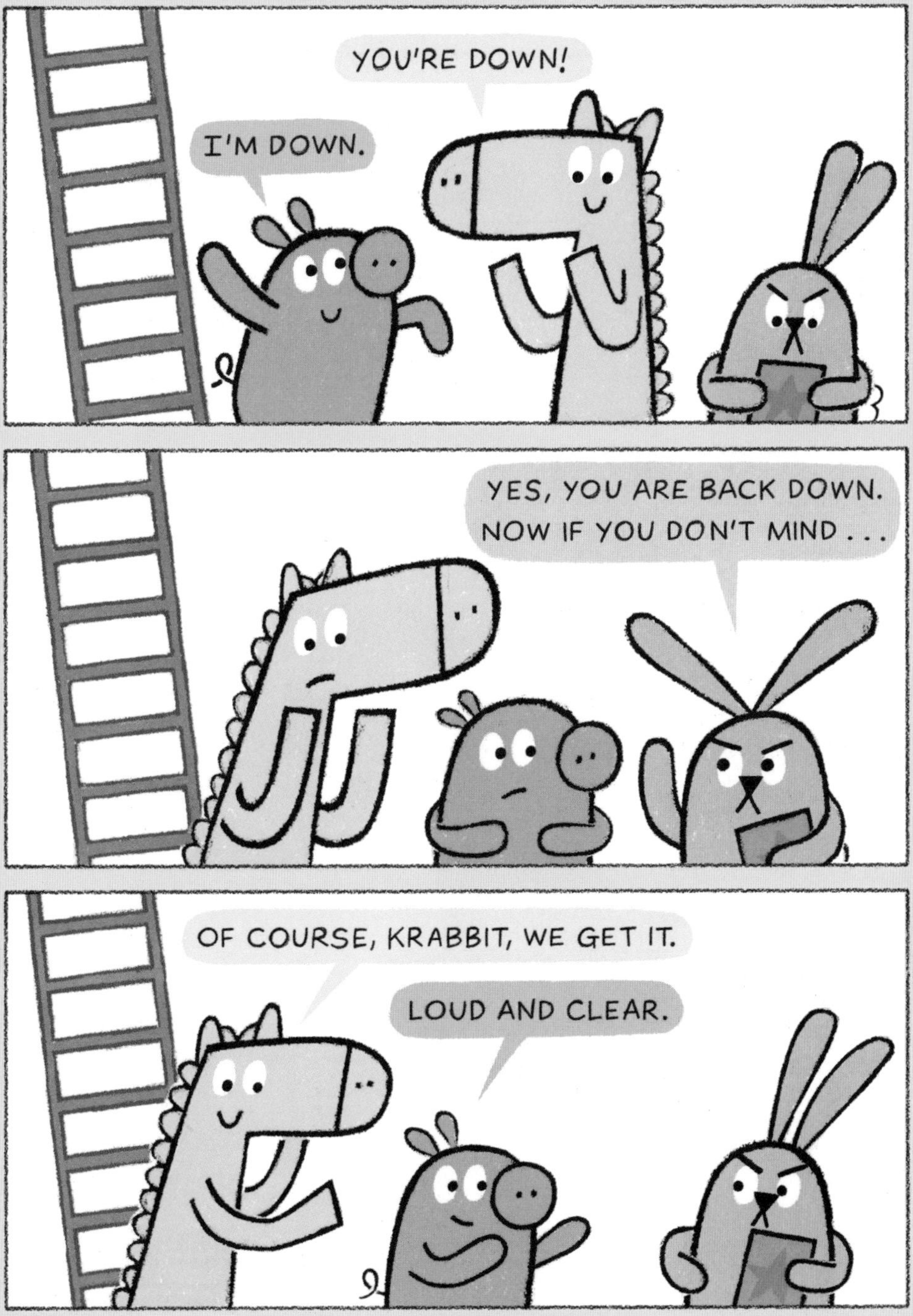
YOU'RE DOWN!
I'M DOWN.
YES, YOU ARE BACK DOWN. NOW IF YOU DON'T MIND . . .
OF COURSE, KRABBIT, WE GET IT.
LOUD AND CLEAR.

46

47

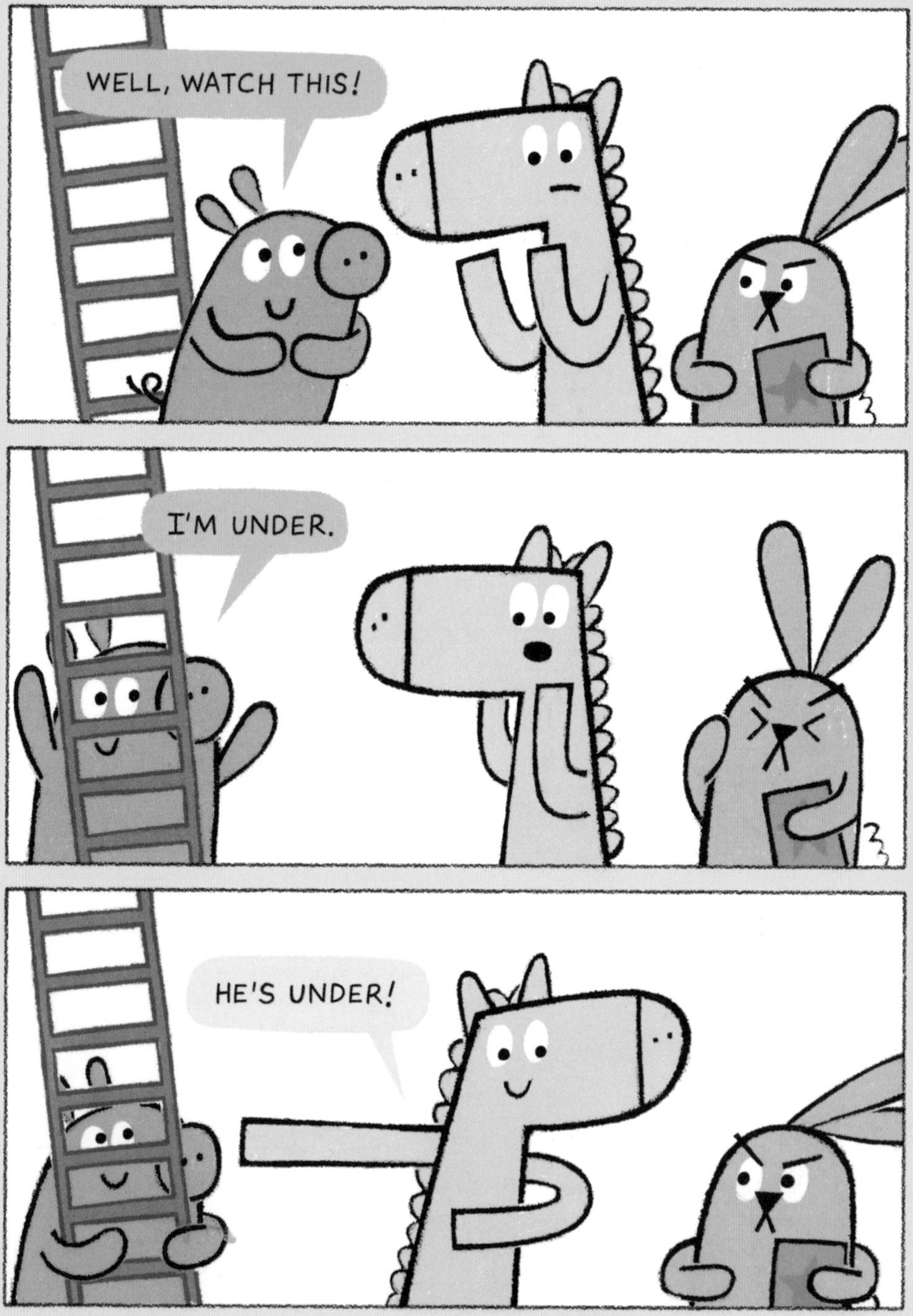
WELL, WATCH THIS!
I'M UNDER.
HE'S UNDER!

49

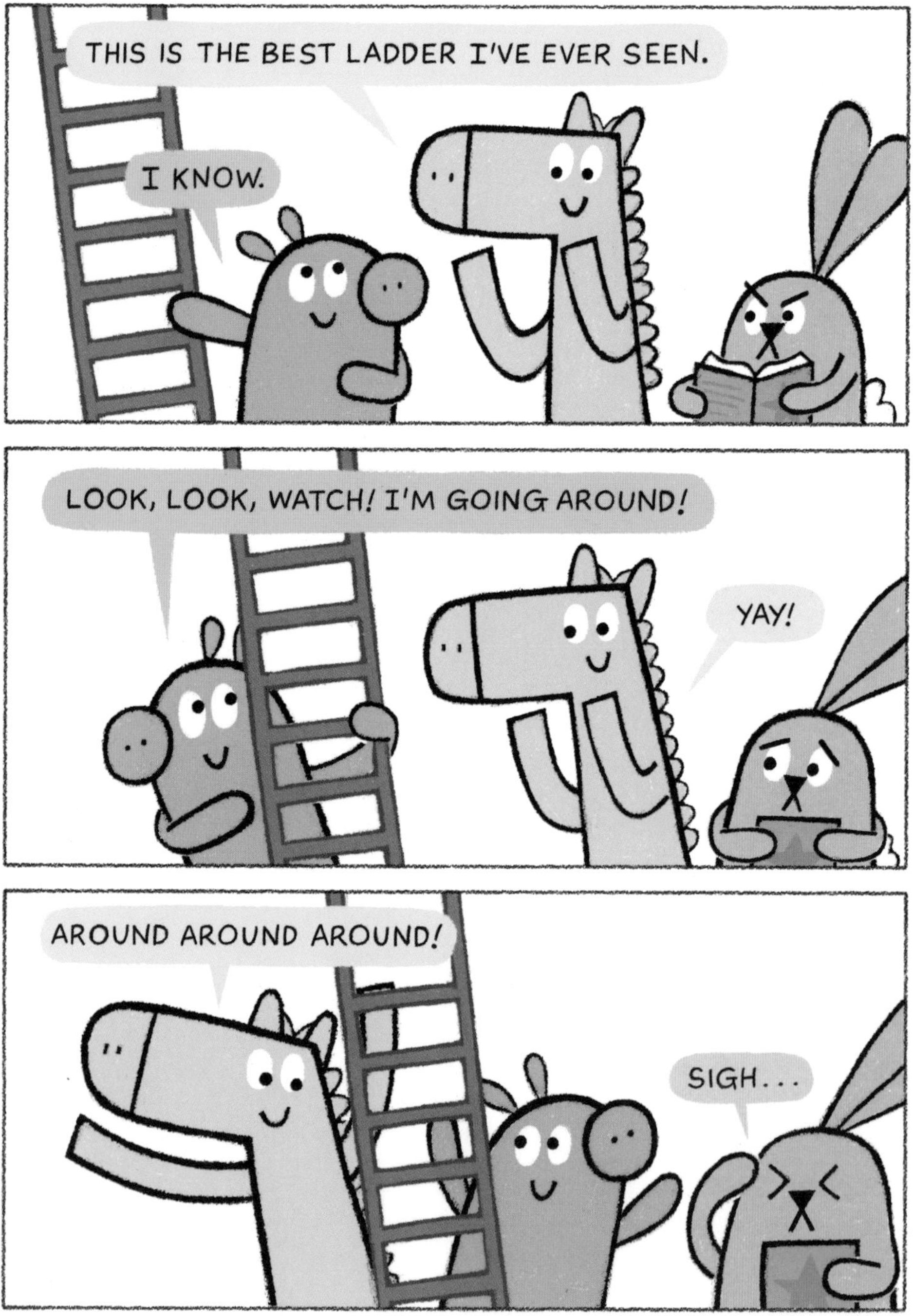
THIS IS THE BEST LADDER I'VE EVER SEEN.
I KNOW.
LOOK, LOOK, WATCH! I'M GOING AROUND!
YAY!
AROUND AROUND AROUND!
SIGH...

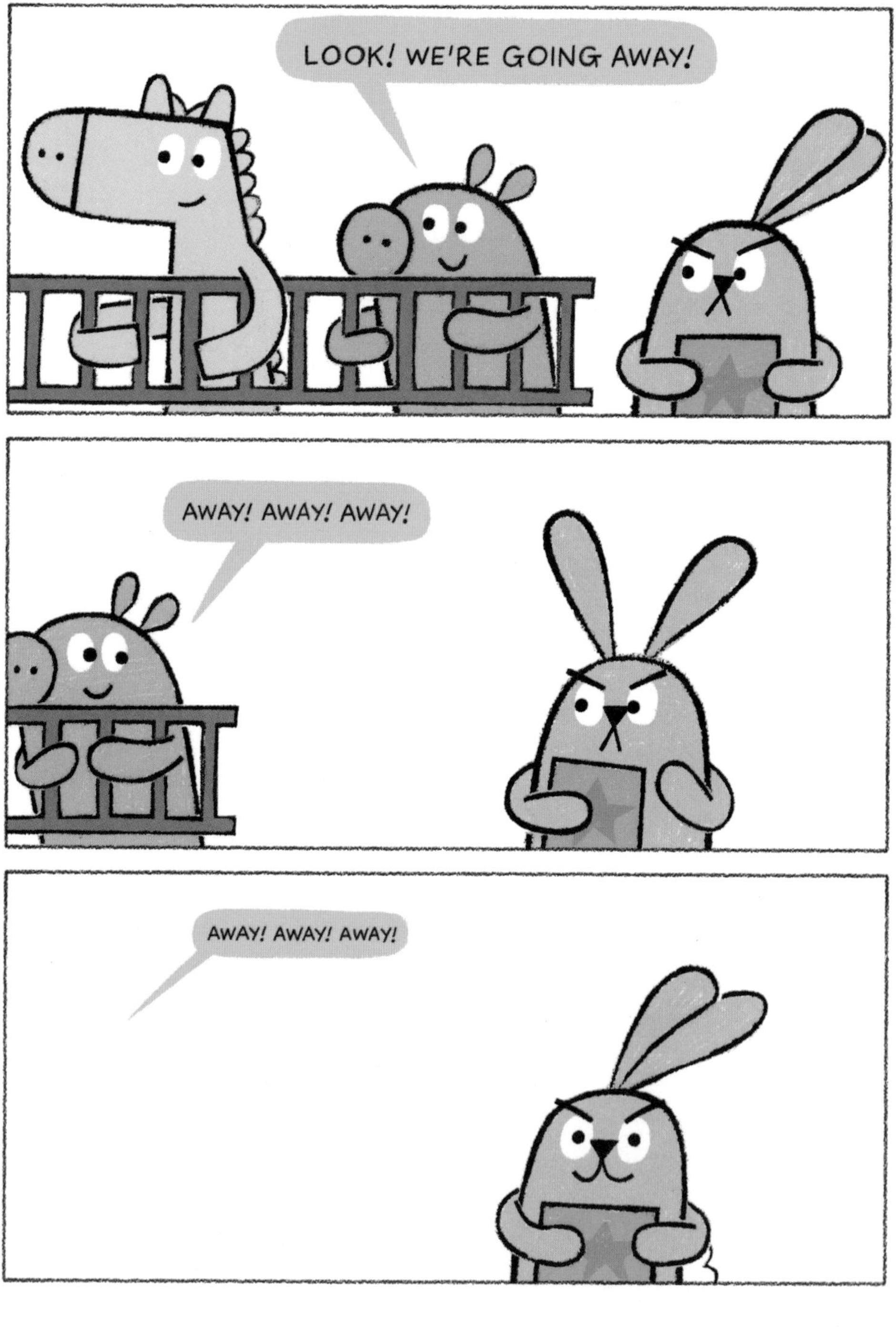
LOOK! WE'RE GOING AWAY!
AWAY! AWAY! AWAY!
AWAY! AWAY! AWAY!

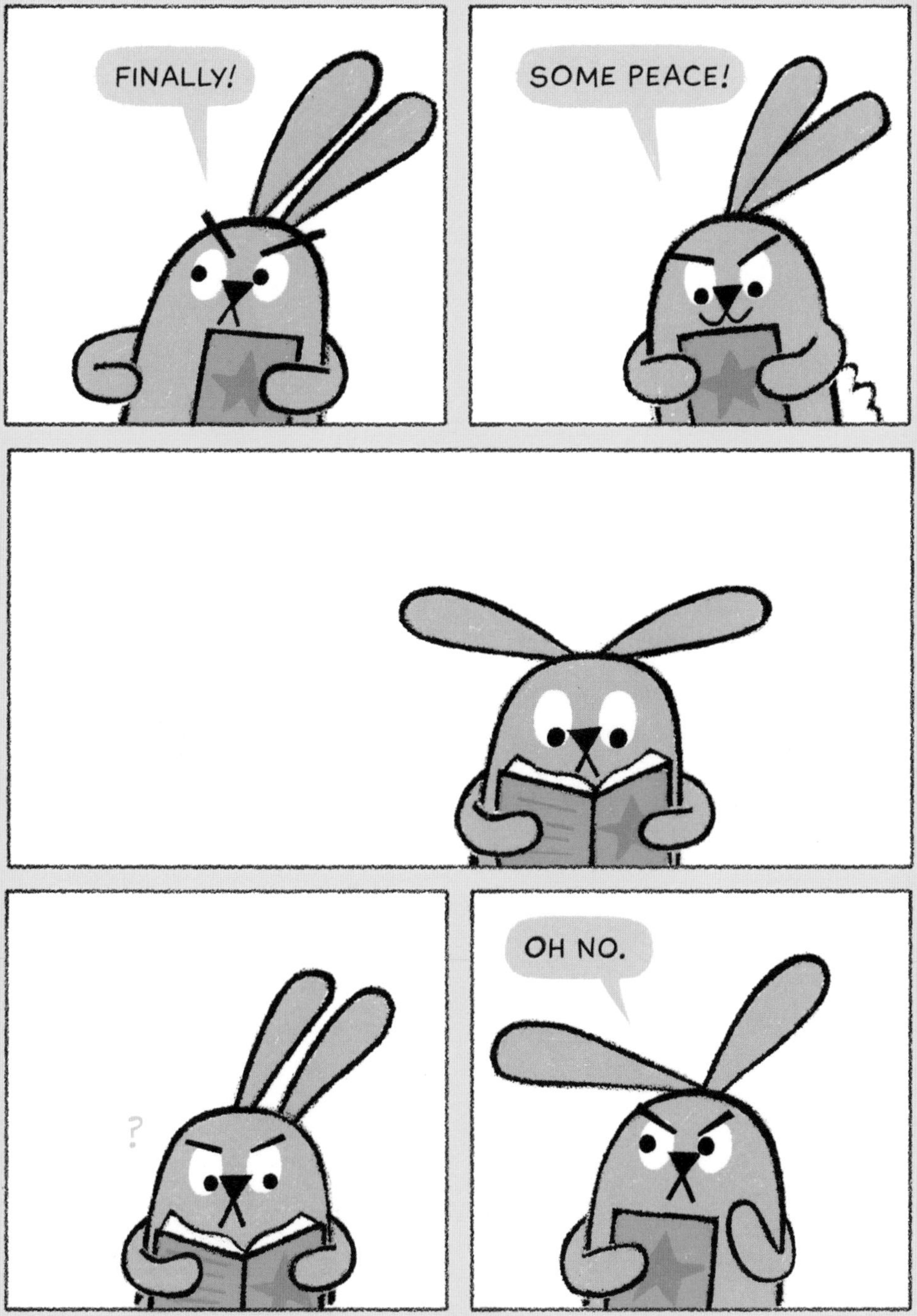
FINALLY!
SOME PEACE!
?
OH NO.

59

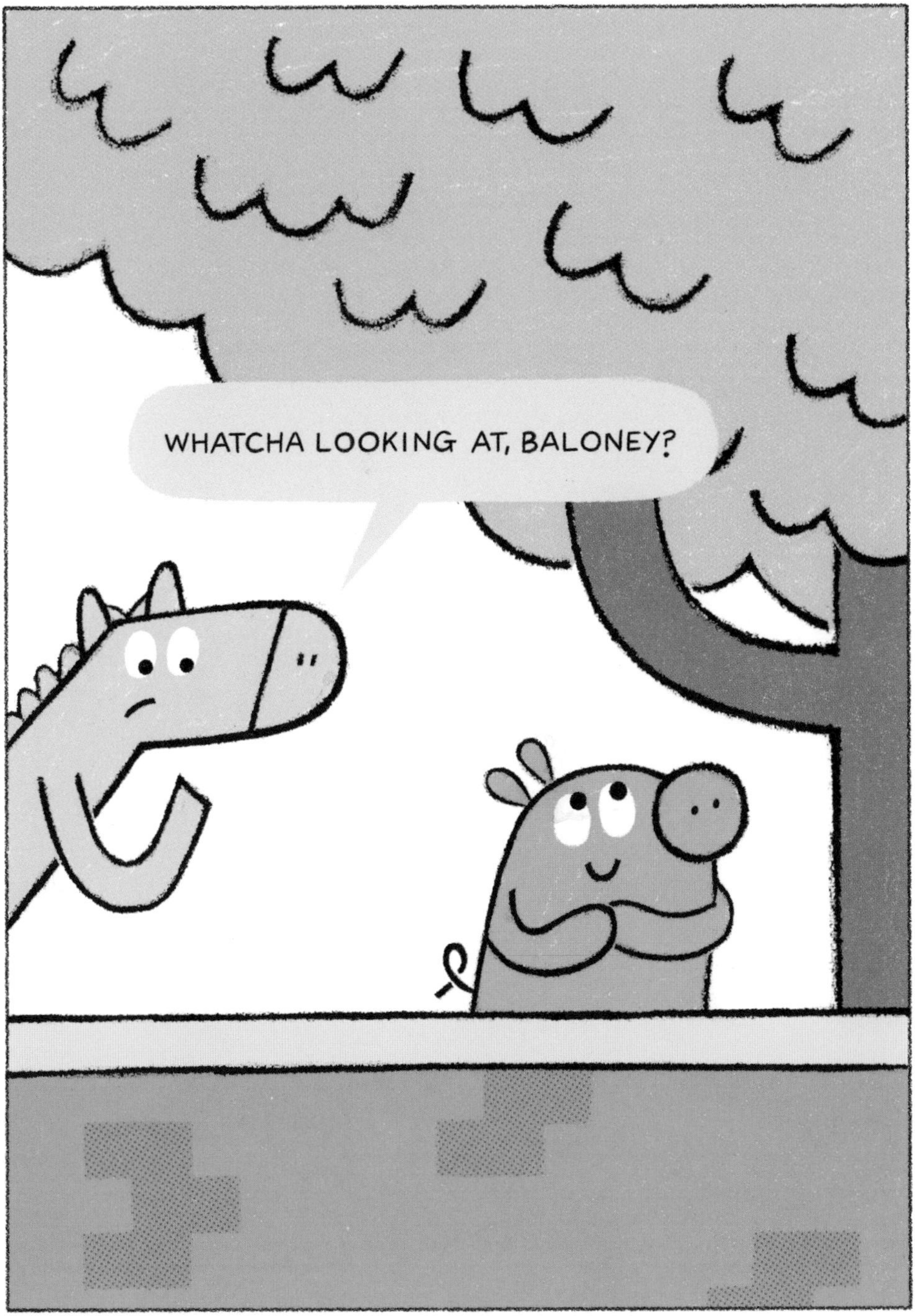
WHATCHA LOOKING AT, BALONEY?

65

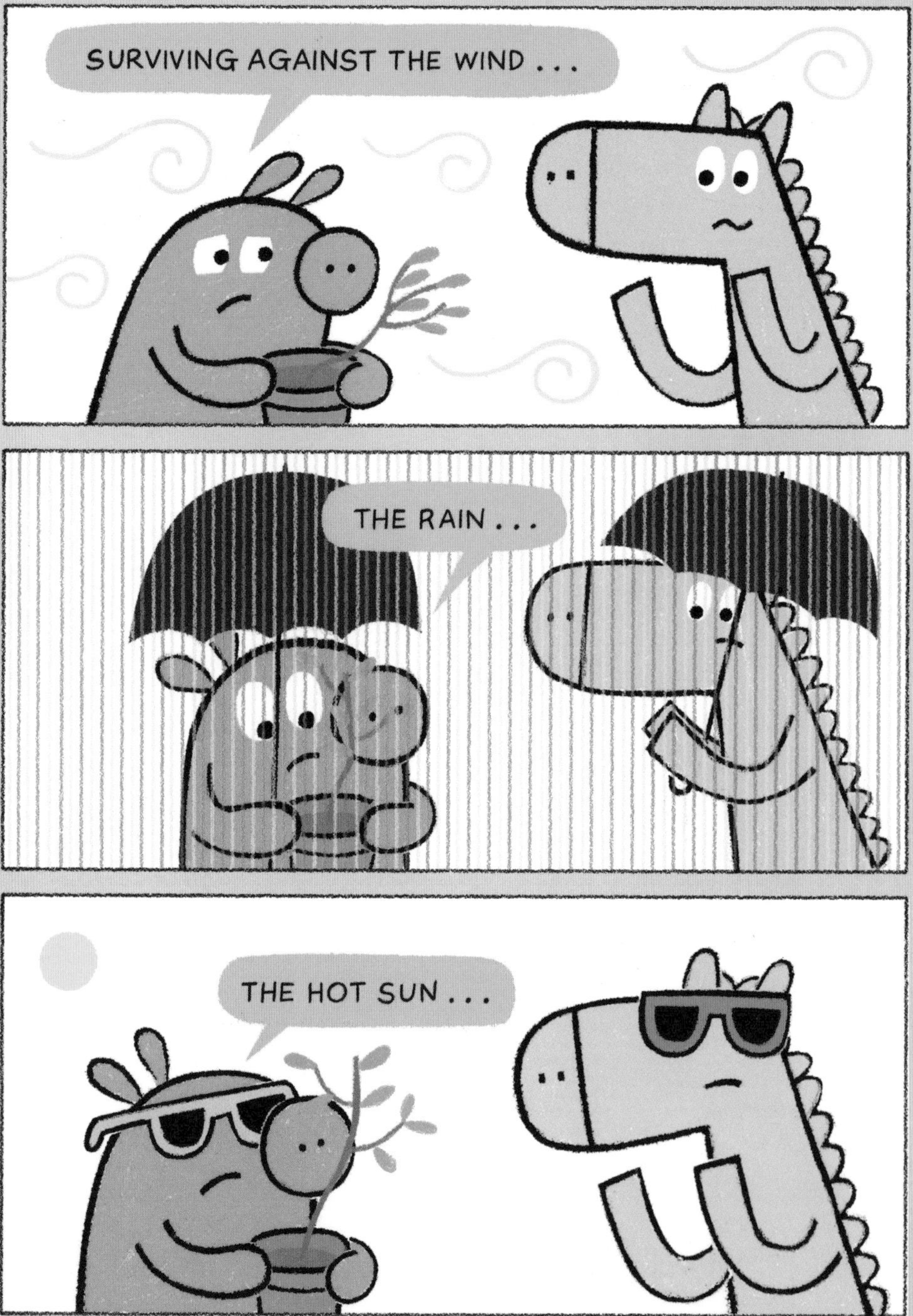
SURVIVING AGAINST THE WIND . . .
THE RAIN . . .
THE HOT SUN . . .

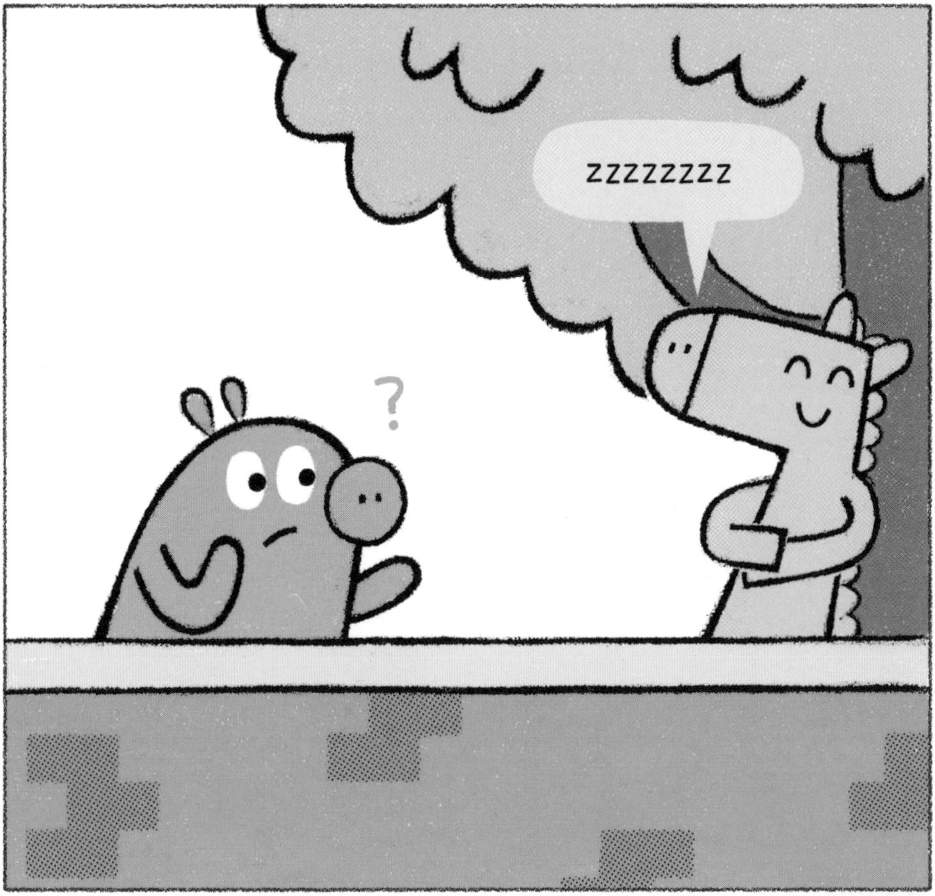
ZZZZZZZZ
?

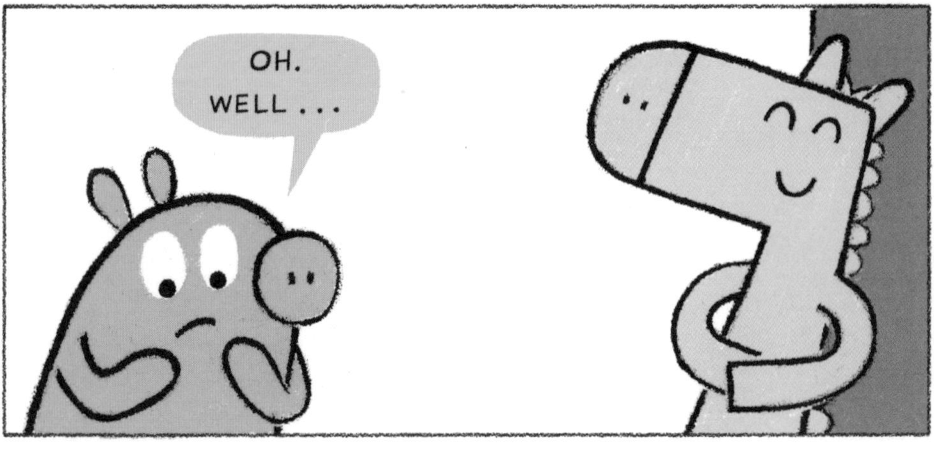
OH.
WELL . . .

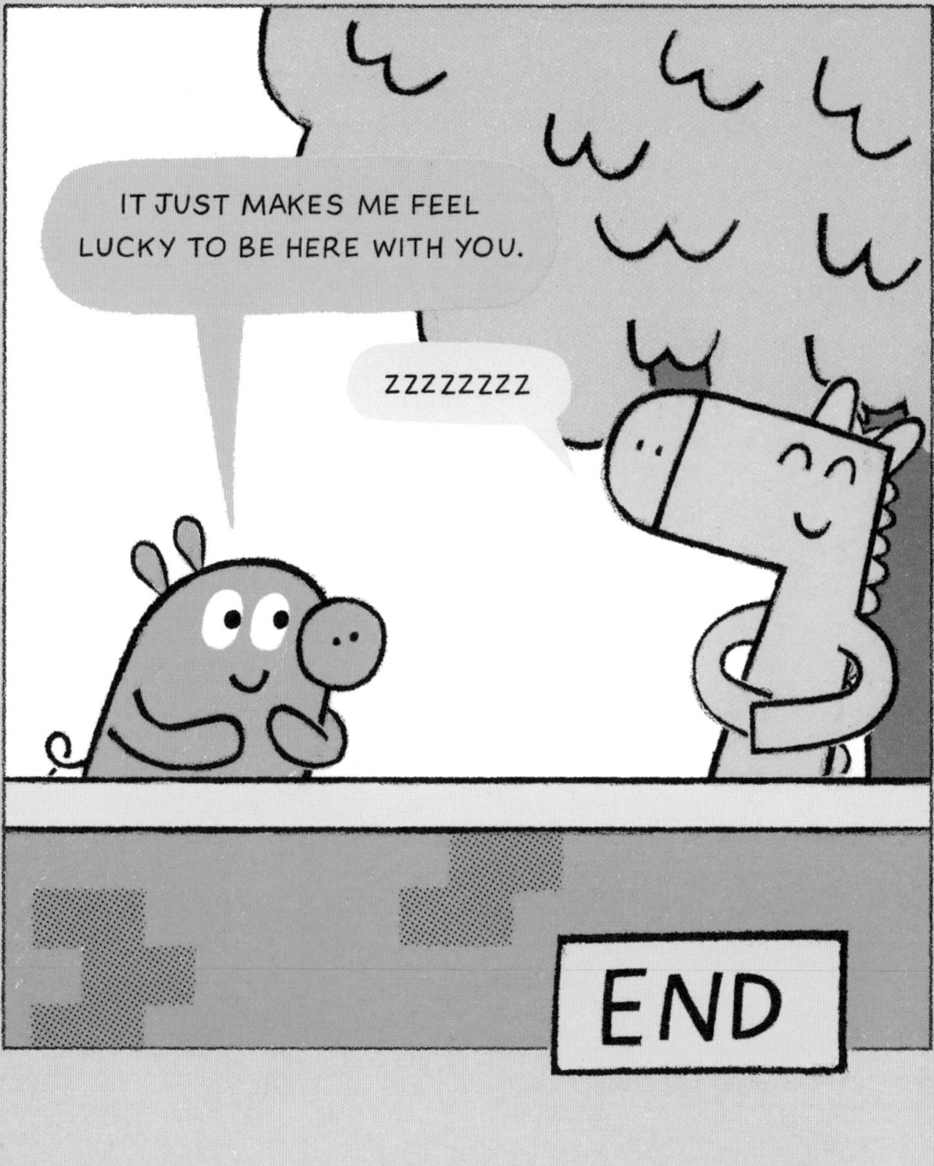
IT JUST MAKES ME FEEL LUCKY TO BE HERE WITH YOU.
ZZZZZZZZ
END

SO LONG, FAREWELL

UNTIL WE MEET AGAIN

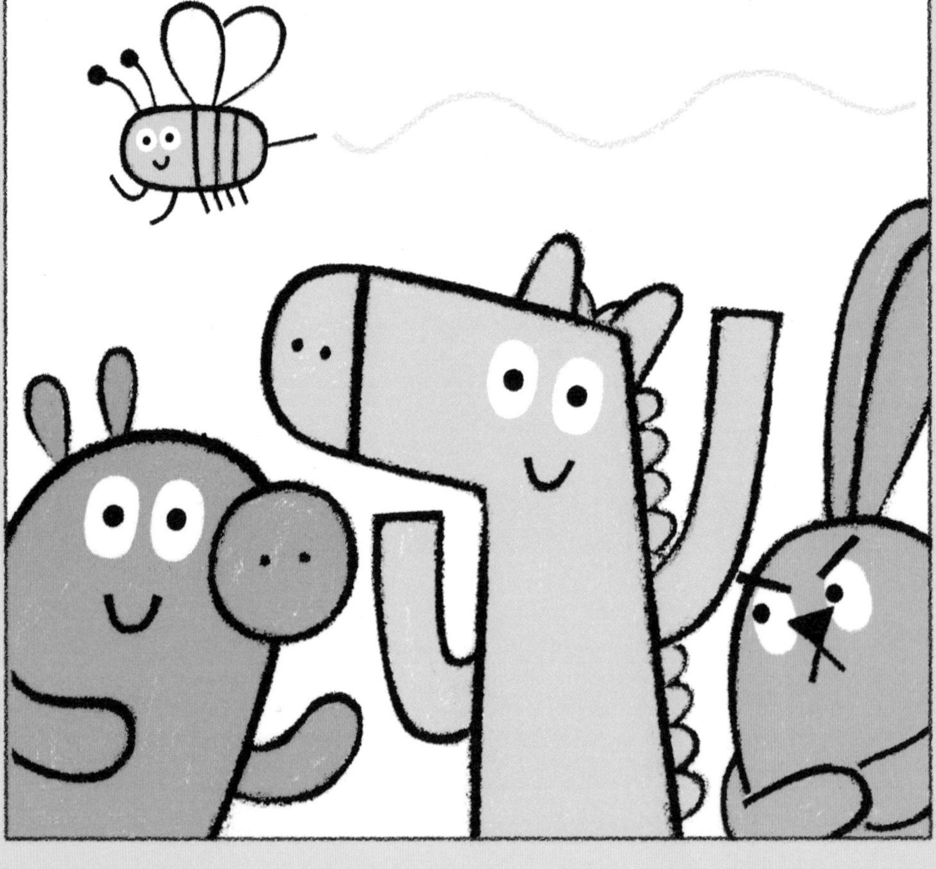

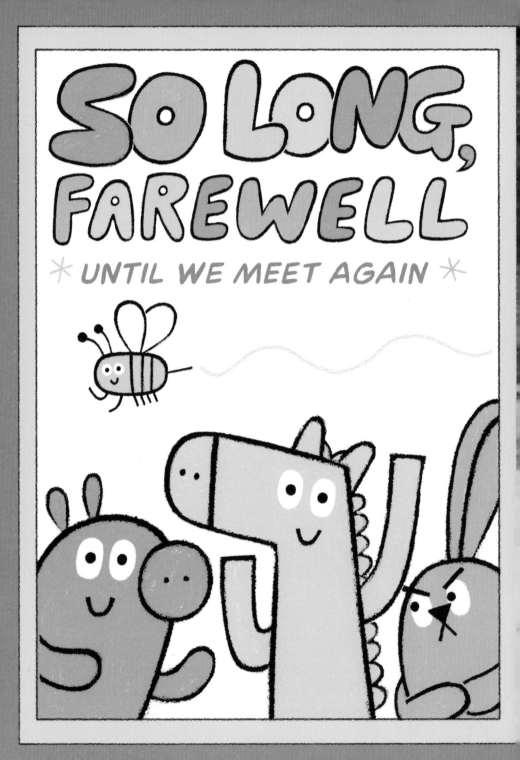

79

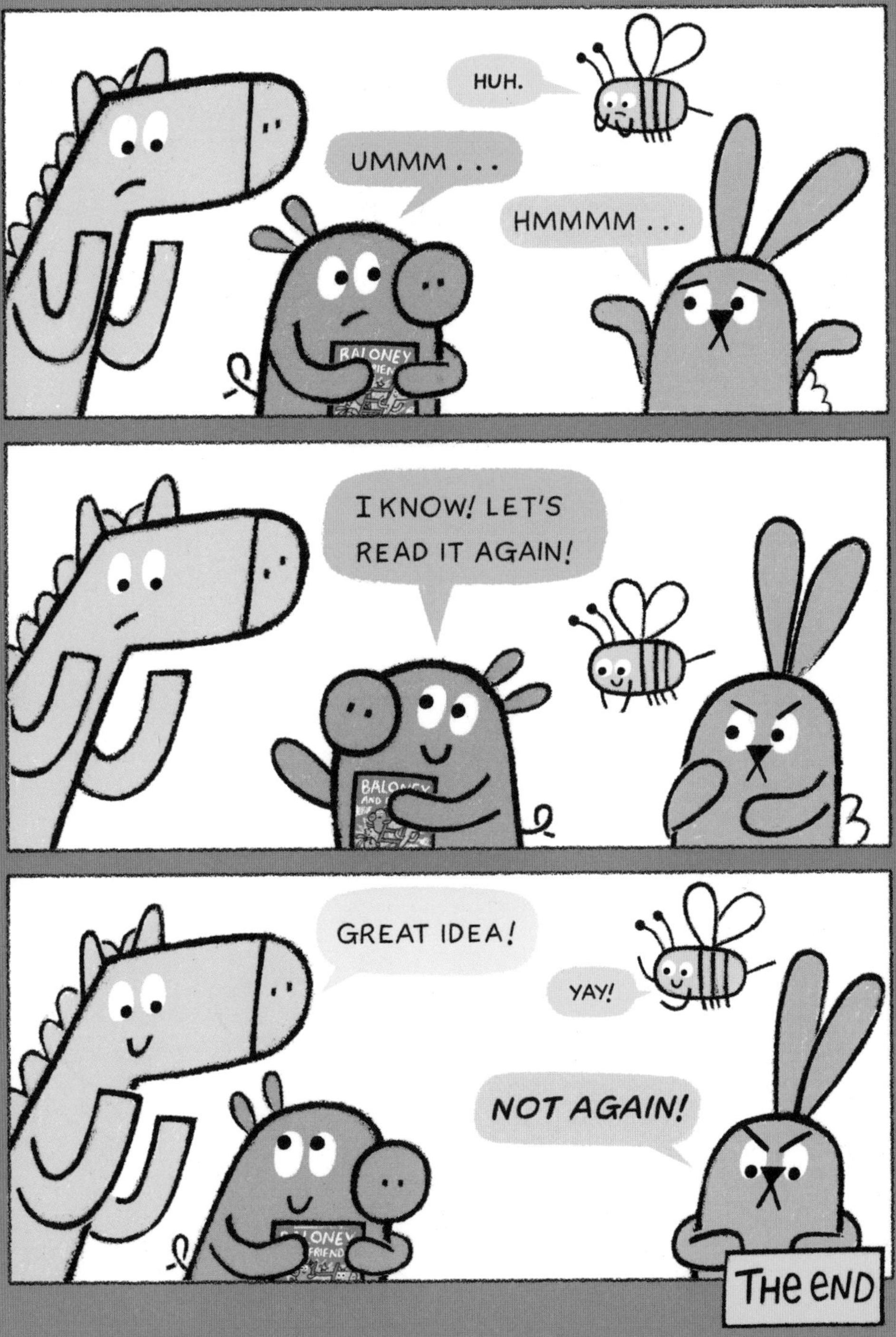
HUH.
UMMM . . .
HMMMM . . .
I KNOW! LET'S READ IT AGAIN!
GREAT IDEA!
YAY!
NOT AGAIN!
THE END

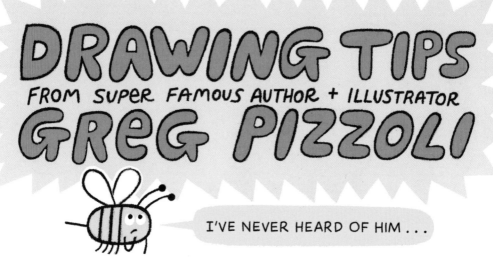

DRAWING TIPS

FROM SUPER FAMOUS AUTHOR + ILLUSTRATOR

GREG PIZZOLI

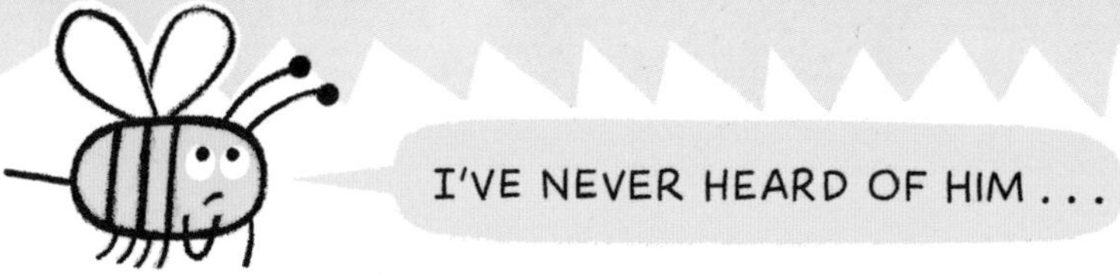
I'VE NEVER HEARD OF HIM . . .

IF YOU ARE MAKING YOUR OWN STORY STARRING BALONEY AND FRIENDS, BE SURE TO GIVE THEM LOTS OF EMOTIONS— IT'S EASY!

YOU CAN EXPERIMENT WITH THE PLACEMENT OF PUPILS, EYEBROWS, SMILES, OR FROWNS— THERE ARE LOTS OF WAYS TO SHOW EMOTION.

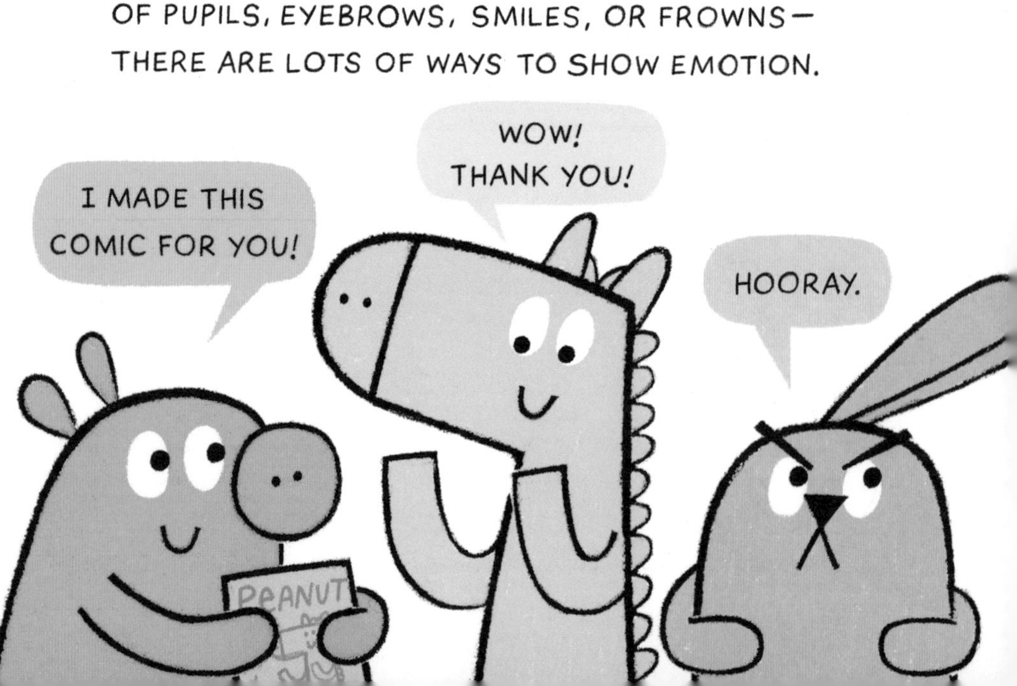
I MADE THIS COMIC FOR YOU!
WOW! THANK YOU!
HOORAY.
PEANUT

NOW GO AND MAKE YOUR OWN COMIC!

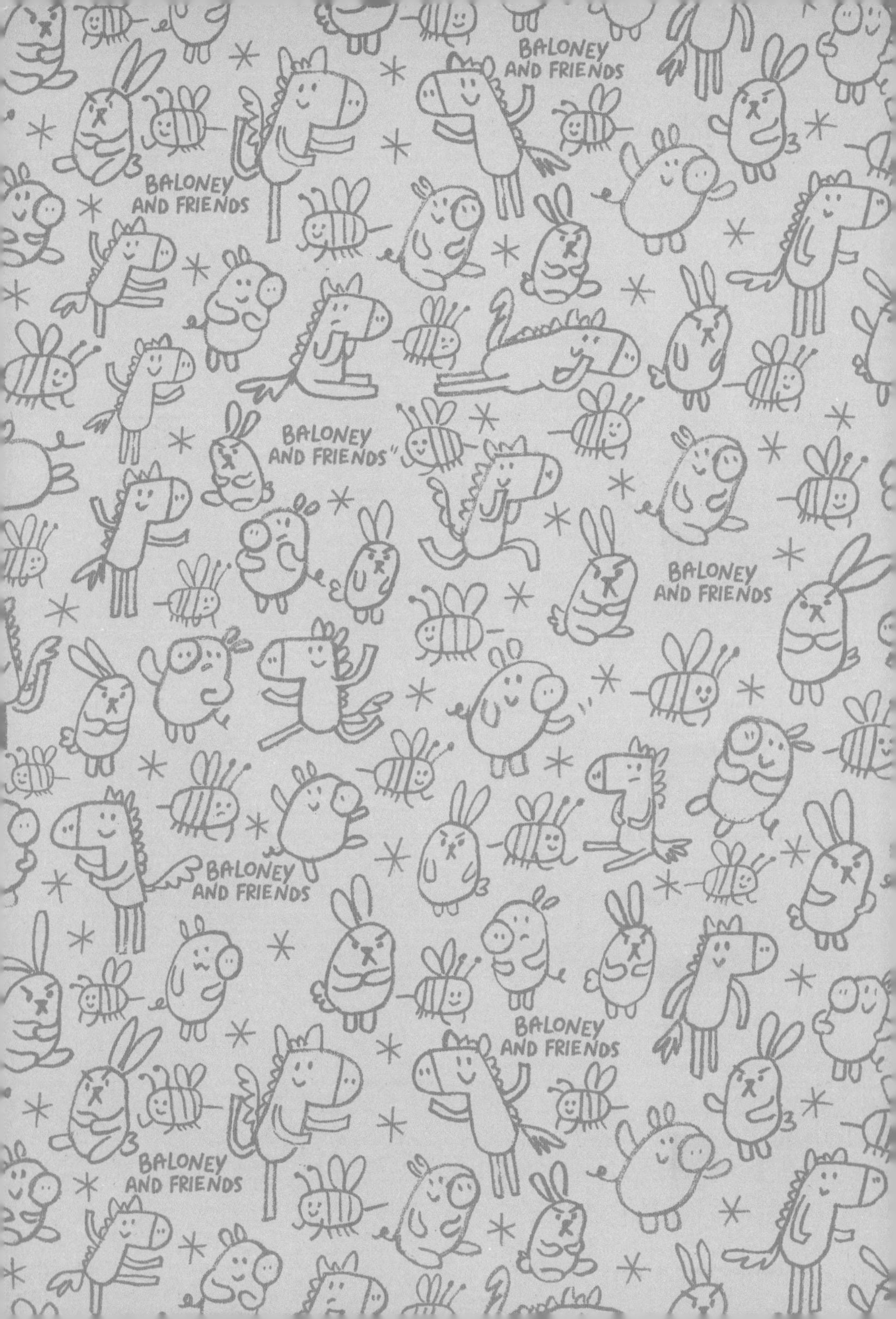
BALONEY AND FRIENDS
BALONEY AND FRIENDS
BALONEY AND FRIENDS
BALONEY AND FRIENDS
BALONEY AND FRIENDS
BALONEY AND FRIENDS
BALONEY AND FRIENDS